MW01626312

American Dystopia

By

Erik Kramer

The Former United States of America

ISBN:

978-1-963679-98-4 **Paperback**

978-1-963679-99-1 **Hardback**

Dedication

I dedicate this book to the countless NCOs that I have worked with throughout the years. Some of them became close friends. Sergeants are the salt of the earth and personify what is best about the U.S. They are what makes the U.S. Army great, and I could count on them to shoot me straight and tell me when "the emperor has no clothes."

I also want to dedicate this book to the soldiers of Ukraine. If you want to see true courage, spend some time with the Armed Forces of Ukraine. Their bravery and courage under fire without all the equipment, training, and support we take for granted in the West is heroic.

Acknowledgments

My daughter, Alexis Kramer, for her advice and encouragement through the years when this book was just an idea in my head and through the editing process.

About the Author

Erik Kramer is the director and cofounder of the Ukraine Defense Support Group (UDSG) located in Kyiv, Ukraine and has been in Ukraine since July 2022, training and advising the Ukrainian Armed Forces. He served in the U.S. Army for 26 years, retiring as a Special Forces lieutenant colonel. Erik has also served as executive director of the nonprofit organization Special Ops Survivors, which provides long-term support to Gold Star spouses of U.S. special operators killed in the line of duty. He was the CEO of Emerging Technology Institute (ETI), a tech company that conducted testing and development on drones, counter-drone, and electronic warfare. He spent many years in the military and out, focusing on emerging threats and hotspots throughout the world, including Asia, Europe, and the Middle East. He has written extensively on national security issues, focusing on Eastern Europe and China. He has a bachelor's of arts degree from The Citadel, the Military College of South Carolina, and a master's of arts degree from the Naval Postgraduate School.

Preface

Are we witnessing the downfall of the United States of America?

To say that we are living in unprecedented times is an understatement. A global pandemic coupled with the most sharply divided the U.S. has been since the Civil War makes our differences seem irreconcilable. One out of five Americans (18%) think violence may be necessary to save the U.S.[1] I have spent the majority of my life defending the American way of life and ideals. It is disheartening to see where we are now.

It feels like we are all in the opening chapters of some dystopian novel. There seems to be a malaise across the entire country that even apolitical people will acknowledge that something is not right and we might be in trouble. This book is a work of fiction and is hopefully just a cautionary tale, not an amateur futurist's road map to our demise.

As a student of history, a former military officer who has worked at senior levels of government, and someone who has traveled far and wide and lived in weak and failed states, my observations are that the U.S. is at a tipping point where if we don't change our trajectory, we could be at the beginning of the end of this great experiment. What follows is a story of how that demise might play out.

---

[1] PRRI Staff, "Competing Visions of America: An Evolving Identity or a Culture Under Attack? Findings from the 2021 American Values Survey," PRRI, accessed on April 18,2024, https://www.prri.org/research/competing-visions-of-america-an-evolving-identity-or-a-culture-under-attack/

Contents

“In these sentiments, Sir, I agree to this Constitution, with all its faults, if they are such, because I think a General Government necessary for us, and there is no form of government, but what may be a blessing to the people if well administered; and believe further, that this is likely to be well administered for years, and can only end in despotism, as other forms have done before it when the people shall become so corrupted as to need despotic government.”

"Well, Doctor (Franklin), what have we got, a republic or a monarchy?"

“A republic, if you can keep it.”

--Benjamin Franklin

September 17, 1787

The last day of the U.S. Constitutional Convention

"This is the way the world ends,

This is the way the world ends,

This is the way the world ends,

Not with a bang but a whimper."

T.S. Eliot

Part 1: How Did We Get Here?

Throughout the annals of human history, the rise and fall of civilizations unveil an often-repeated tale of powerful empires ascending to great heights only to succumb to the weight of their demise. How have they collapsed? Usually, it is from internal rot and strife. It starts with a loss of trust in institutions, a loss in civility amongst the populace, tribalism, corruption, and a loss of the "ties that bind" society.

Suppose you look at the major empires throughout history: the Romans, Egyptians, Mayans, the Ottomans, the Byzantines, the Austro-Hungarian Empire, the British Empire, and the Soviet Union. They all follow a similar pattern. The turmoil starts on the periphery of the Empire at the same time, the internal problems commence.

Every Empire likes to think it is different. When you look at the two modern Empires which proceeded the U.S., the Soviet Union and the British Empire, it started with the inability to control its holdings or interests abroad. In the case of the Soviet Union, Afghanistan proved to be the "graveyard" of its demise. It showed that the Soviet Union was not all-powerful if a country such as Afghanistan, with the technology of the Middle Ages, could defeat them. The growing casualties caused dissension and turmoil back home, especially with the mothers of the soldiers killed.[2] The British Empire slowly collapsed not from corruption but from overreach on its periphery and World War II. The United Kingdom did experience internal economic turmoil post World War II that made the idea of an expensive Empire hard to justify. Also, after the War, there was a post-colonialism movement.

The U.S. has been the reluctant Empire and world policeman. It tried to leave the world stage before after World War I but was dragged back into a costly world war. The U.S. likes to say it is the exception; think American hubris and exceptionalism, but every Empire thinks it is the "chosen one" and is smarter than the others. One could arguably trace the U.S.'s "periphery problems" to the forever wars in Afghanistan and Iraq. In both of these conflicts, the U.S. lost the "will of the

---

[2] 2004. Julie Elkner. Dedovshchina and the Committee of Soldiers' Mothers under Gorbachev. https://journals.openedition.org/pipss/243

people" and had many Americans questioning why we were spending so many lives and so much treasure on wars that had lost meaning and with no end in sight.

So, what brought us together and has kept us together?

I would argue that is the "idea of America", our constant turnover of our populace, and our unrelenting pursuit of capitalism. The late 20th-century view of America is that anyone can make it here as long as you follow the rules and work hard. You can keep your traditions, culture, and religion; just allow others to do the same. In addition, we have constantly had a refreshing of the American "gene pool" through immigration. I will say that the acceptance of immigrants in America is a fallacy and a myth. I have traveled the world and I am often asked, why is it so hard to immigrate to the U.S.? I call it the "America is closed for business after my people get in" approach, an immigration version of "not in my backyard (NIMBY)". Suppose you look at the history of the U.S. In that case, groups of immigrants, such as the Irish, Italians, Chinese, etc., arrive in massive waves, are discriminated against, and then, once they are established and fully assimilated, want the door shut on subsequent groups. So, the U.S.'s "melting pot" is achieved despite our best efforts to impede it. Then we throw capitalism into the mix, and you have what drives us.

Nobody does capitalism like the U.S. Just look at the legal marijuana business compared to a place like the Netherlands, where it has been semi-legal for decades. If you walk into any marijuana dispensary in the U.S., the sheer volume of choices can be overwhelming. Compared to the Netherlands, where it is still almost a cottage industry. If the world's problems could be solved by applying capitalism to every situation, we would run out of problems quickly. It is our strength and our weakness. In our drive to succeed, make money, make the lives of our children better than ours, and follow our passions, culture, and "tribe", Americans easily become insulated and isolated. We only focus on what is immediately important to us, and most of us have only a superficial interest or understanding of the world outside of the U.S. Our information flow ends up being in a closed-loop system, where our sources of information are tailored to reinforce our believes, whether it is through the sources of news we watch or the people we spend the most time with. It is a false paradigm.

No competing views or opinions are present to question our thoughts, so our views become hardened and entrenched. I remember coming back from a trip to Ukraine in 2016. When I told a new acquittance where I had been, she asked if Ukraine was part of the Soviet Union. Again, our pursuit of capitalistic success is our strength and our weakness. It causes us to be so inwardly focused that, at times, we do not understand some of the biggest international issues of the day, but the problem is that we think we understand.

Part 2: And What Is Breaking Us Apart?

Forests have been decimated, explaining why we are at each other's throats. I will not go into details here, but from years of experience in failed/failing states, it is a lot of the reasons that I already mentioned, loss of trust in each other and our institutions and the villainization of our fellow citizens. If there is one root reason for our current situation, it is the internet and the explosion of unfiltered information. Before the internet, information flow was mainly restricted to professional journalists, writers, and government officials. Newspapers, network news, and government-issued press releases ruled the day. The news was the realm of the professionals. The average American had limited sources of information, and they were from generally credible sources. In the 70s and 80s, the U.S. only had four main TV channels, and there was no 24/7 news.

If the sources of information turned out to be wrong or false, there was such a limited amount of information compared to today that it could be debated, researched, refuted, or questioned in the court of public opinion without the debate becoming overwhelmed by the sheer volume of information and the din of the loudest voices.

Now, our strengths have become our weaknesses, i.e., focusing on our personal success, life, problems, culture, and tribe. Our news is not filtered and vetted like it was pre-internet. Unfortunately, our personal information filters have not changed, but the volume and quality of information and news have completely changed for the worse. As a result, many of our fellow Americans are confusing the loudest voice or the opinion, what we agree with the most, or what our tribal consensus is as the truth. That is very dangerous in a democracy where the power is supposed to reside with the people and is based on a system of trust in each other and our institutions. Now, everything is called into question.

What follows is a cautionary tale of the collapse of the U.S., using real-world events and people as much as possible. I strived to keep it as realistic as possible based on such things as how our Constitutional Amendments regarding Presidential succession work and how our government functions. This book, short story, or whatever category it fits into started as a work on nonfiction, but after several paragraphs of typing "what if" scenarios, I realized that writing a historical fiction novel might be the best way to convey these ideas and concepts. Also, if I showed how the collapse affected individuals, from government officials to Americans across the country, the reader could get a better sense of the repercussions of a collapse and how its effects would permeate almost every aspect of American life.

UN Study on the Collapse of the U.S.

This historical document represents the most in-depth study of the collapse of the United States of America, including the slow buildup, the turmoil, chaos, and violence that followed. It is the culmination of thousands of hours of interviews with current politicians and former U.S. politicians in the various mini-states that now make up the territory that was formerly known as the U.S., the media, TV personalities, military, law enforcement, political scientists, and ordinary citizens.

Timeline: The path to collapse

- **January-February 2024**: Texas Governor Abbott refuses to obey a Supreme Court ruling that the U.S. Border Guards can remove border obstacles he had placed.[3] Republican Governors support Governor Abbott's refusal, and many send their own National Guardsmen.[4]
- **May 2024**: Grassroots write-in campaign with Michael Jordan as a Presidential candidate and General and former Secretary of Defense "Bulldog" Matthis as a Vice Presidential candidate goes viral. It initially started because of frustration over the unpopularity of the two main candidates, Donald Trump and President Joe Biden. Based on the varied state laws for write-in candidates, they are eligible for write-in in 42 states and the District of Columbia. Initially, both candidates dismissed their candidacies until their popularity led them to develop a platform and start campaigning. They combined efforts with the "No Labels" grassroots organization. Matthis was seen as the experienced government hand as well as a former Republican who could help Michael Jordan, who has never held elected office. Michael touts his business expertise as well as his centrist views. He states that "the people have spoken, and given all of the turmoil and divisiveness that has gone on in our country, it would be beyond negligent of me not to try and bring us back together. When

[3] Olivia Alafriz and Christine Zhu, "Supreme Court allows border agents to remove razor wire in Texas," *Politico*, January 22, 2024, https://www.politico.com/news/2024/01/22/supreme-court-allows-border-agents-to-remove-razor-wire-in-texas-00137059

[4] Nick Mordowanec, "GOP Governors Have Already Sent Troops to Texas Amid 'Civil War' Fears," *Newsweek*, January 26, 2024, https://www.newsweek.com/gop-governors-troops-texas-civil-war-fears-border-1864435

your neighborhood is on fire, you grab a bucket." They promise to form a unity government of officials from both parties and outside of government that is centrist left on social issues and centrist right on foreign policy and the economy. Their campaign slogan is "Unity and Common Cause".

Potential members of their cabinet include Amazon CEO Jeff Bezos, businessman Warren Buffet, former U.S. Congresswoman from Wyoming Liz Cheney-Republican, former founder and CEO of Microsoft Bill Gates, Georgia Governor Brian Kemp-Republican, former First Lady Michelle Obama, former U.S. Senator Mitt Romney from Utah-Republican, U.S. Senator Bernie Sanders from Vermont-Independent, former Governor of California Arnold Schwarzenegger-Republican, and Michigan Governor Gretchen Whitmer-Democrat. Both Governors Kemp and Whitmer state that it is well past time to put the country above the party.

- **August 2024**: President Biden falls and suffers a severe concussion. Controversy reigns about whether the Vice President and Cabinet should enact the 25th Amendment. President Biden recovers, but not before impeachment hearings take place in Congress over his fitness to continue serving as the President.
- **October 2024**: Former President Trump was found guilty of nine of the 13 charges of election tampering by the state of Georgia. Sentencing places, him under house arrest for 18 months. In a separate federal trial, he was also found guilty in three out of the four federal charges of two counts of obstruction and one count of conspiracy to defraud the U.S. and sentenced to two years of house arrest followed by a year of probation.[5] Trump supporters in all 50 states protested, claiming that the decisions were politically motivated and the outcomes of the trials were intentionally coordinated so they would come out right before the November election. There is an unsuccessful assassination attempt against the lead federal prosecutor three days after the jury's decision.
- **November 2024-January 2025**: Presidential elections violently protested. In some places, voting was suspended due to the level of violence and bombings. The new Unity party splits the vote, and as a result, no party has 270 electoral votes, The 12th Amendment goes

[5] Tracking the Trump criminal cases," Politico, updated April 15, 2024, https://www.politico.com/interactives/2023/trump-criminal-investigations-cases-tracker-list/.

into effect, House and Senate will decide the election results.[6] Protests break out in every state, and some turn violent. The new Republican House, which is responsible for electing the President under the 12th Amendment, cannot reach a clear majority by January 20 as dictated in the 20th Amendment.[7] The Senate, with a one Senator majority, elects Kamala Harris as the Vice President. Under the rules of the 12th and 20th Amendments, when the House is unable to reach a majority agreement by January 20, the Vice President-elect, Kamala Harris, becomes the acting President. A constitutional crisis ensues, and the matter goes to the Supreme Court for a decision. The Supreme Court declined to make a ruling, stating that this matter is best left to the Constitution and the voters.

The day after the Supreme Court declined to make a ruling, a bomb threat was called into the Supreme Court. During the evacuation, a swarm of hundreds of kamikaze drones overwhelmed Washington, DC air defenses established after September 11 and attacked the underground parking garage where the Supreme Court Justices were about to evacuate. The garage collapses, killing the entire U.S. Supreme Court. It takes days to remove the rubble and determine that there are no survivors.

Violent protests break out nationwide in most major cities. Pro-Trump protestors clash with pro-Biden/Harris supporters. President Harris is sworn in as the 51st President of the U.S. at 11:30 pm on January 20, 2025. She immediately delivers a nationwide, primetime address invoking the Insurrection Act of 1807 and federalizing the National Guard in states with violent protests and uprisings. Governors in several Republican-led states refused to federalize their National Guard forces, stating that President Harris was not duly elected as the President, so her order was illegal and unconstitutional.

- **February 2025**: Idaho state assembly votes to secede from the U.S. and immediately announces that it is now the independent country of Idaho. The states of Texas, Ohio, South Carolina, Alabama, Tennessee, Louisiana, North Carolina, Georgia, and West Virginia voted to secede as well. A Constitutional crisis ensues. There is no longer a sitting Supreme

[6] "Amdt.12.1 Overview of the Twelfth Amendment," Cornell Law School, Legal Information Institute, accessed May 5, 2024, https://www.law.cornell.edu/constitution-conan/amendment-12/overview-of-the-twelfth-amendment.
[7] "Twentieth Amendment: Doctrine and Practice," Cornell Law School, Legal Information Institute, accessed May 5, 2024, https://www.law.cornell.edu/constitution-conan/amendment-20/twentieth-amendment-doctrine-and-practice.

Court, so the next lower court, the U.S. Court of Appeals, issued conflicting rulings. The Federal Court in Washington, DC, the Second and the Seventh Circuits rule that it is unconstitutional for states to secede from the Union, citing the Civil War as precedence. The Fifth and 11th Circuits, who earlier had ruled that President Harris was not duly elected, rule that states have a right to secede when the federal government is unable to perform its Constitutional duties. Standoffs occur between National Guardsmen and state police on one side and active military on the other in seceded states at large military bases, including Ft. Liberty, NC, Ft. Campbell, KY, and Ft. Cavazos, TX, just to name a few. The first military mutiny takes place in Texas. Violence breaks out in several states, including Georgia, Illinois, North Carolina, and northern California.

- **March 2025**: Arkansas, Illinois, Kentucky, Montana, North Dakota, Oklahoma, South Dakota, and Wyoming secede from the U.S.

  March-April 2025: Violence escalates in Chicago in protest of the secession from the U.S. It becomes a standoff between the state government of Illinois against the government and the people of Chicago. Chicago is basically under siege and surrounded by Illinois National Guard and Illinois State Police.
- **March 2, 2025**: The Oakland City Massacre in Atlanta, GA, takes place. Members of the Georgia National Guard killed 38 mainly young black men and women. Both sides claim that the other started shooting first. It is considered the starting point for the full-fledged insurgency ongoing in Atlanta.
- **April 2025**: Florida, Indiana, Kansas, Mississippi, Missouri, Nebraska, and Iowa secede.
- **April 4, 2025**: Several states in the southeast (Alabama, Georgia, Louisiana, North Carolina, South Carolina, and Tennessee) declare the formation of a new country, the United States of the South.
- **May 10, 2025**: The rogue nuclear weapons-carrying U.S. Navy submarine, USS Alabama, is sunk off of the coast of Cuba. The captain had refused to obey recall orders in February and threatened to launch his nuclear missiles onboard.
- **May 26, 2025**: A bombing at the Memorial Day Coca-Cola 600 NASCAR race in Charlotte, NC, killed 219 attendees and injured over 500 others. An anonymous social media post claims that the bombing took place because of the illegal secession of the Southern states and the killing of black people in Atlanta by National Guardsmen.

- **May 29, 2025**: The states of Montana, North Dakota, South Dakota, and Wyoming announce the formation of the Mountain Empire.
- **June 2025**: Colorado, Nevada, Utah, and Wisconsin secede. Over half the states in the U.S. have seceded and recalled their Congressional delegations. The only contiguously bordering states that have not been located are from Virginia to Maine. California, in a legal sleight of hand, states that it is not seceding, but because the federal government is unable to provide necessary services, it is temporarily assuming the duties of the federal government within its borders. Oregon and Washington state agreed to pool their resources with California.
- **July 2025**: The eastern counties in Oregon and Washington that border Idaho declare their independence from those two states and join with Idaho. The Nevada counties that border California vote to join California. A full-blown insurgency is now taking place in northern California and southern Oregon in the area of the self-declared Republic of Jefferson.
- **August 2025**: Arkansas, Oklahoma, and Texas announce the formation of Texarkana.
- **August 24, 2025**: In a statewide referendum, Minnesotans vote to enter into talks with Canada about an EU-like relationship.
- **December 2025**: Explosion at port facilities in Jacksonville, FL, releases radioactive material. It is a dirty bomb, but the political fallout results in Florida withdrawing from the U.S.S. Insurgency groups in Georgia and North Carolina claiming responsibility.
- **February 2026**: Utah declares its independence and that it is now a sovereign country.
- **2025-2026:** Several former U.S. states have ongoing violent conflicts within their borders that each state is handling differently. Several former states form their governments as groups of former states or independently (see below for the breakdown). The rump U.S. nation-state still exists but encompasses only the U.S. states in the northeast (Connecticut, Delaware, Maine, Maryland, Massachusetts, New Hampshire, New Jersey, New York, Rhode Island, Vermont, and Virginia).
- **November 2026:** The states in what remains of the U.S. amend the U.S. Constitution to recognize the new realities and to create a legal framework for the states that seceded. The Amendment gives the green light for the states that have not officially left the Union to secede. All states outside of the contiguous rump state that is now the new U.S. have seceded.

- **December 2026**: California, Oregon, and Washington announce the former of the United West Coast Federation.
    - Arizona, Colorado, and New Mexico announce the formation of the Independent States of the West.
    - Minnesota declares its independence and enters negotiations with Canada to form an EU-like agreement with them.
    - Indiana, Illinois, Michigan, Ohio, and Wisconsin formed the Don't Tread on Me Confederation.
    - Alaska and Hawaii declare that they are now independent countries. Despite the distance, they have entered into an agreement where their economies are intertwined.

January 2027: The former states of Iowa, Kansas, Missouri, and Nebraska form the Farm Belt Coalition.

2027: Present day.

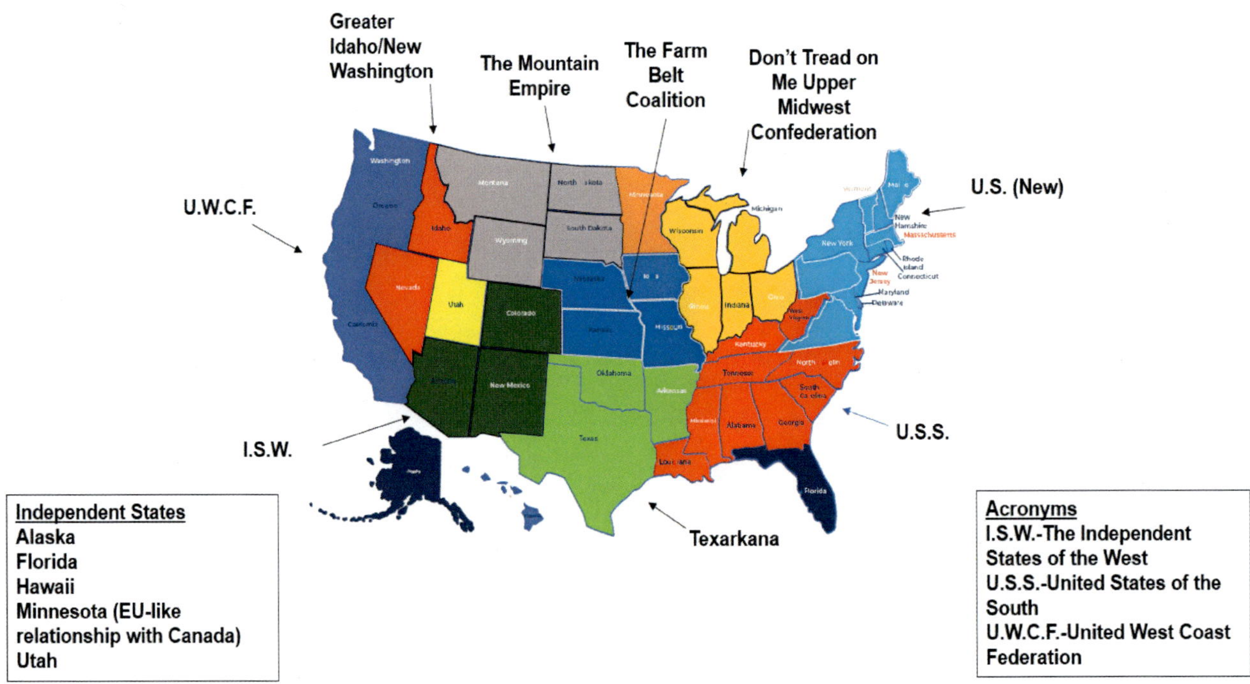

Current independent countries or confederations that make up the territory formally known as the United States of America (areas that are still in dispute, whether peacefully or still in armed conflict, are noted):

COLOR CODES

BLACK- Former state is in armed conflict

INDEPENDENT- Former state has declared its path

RED- Former states are right-leaning

BLUE- Former states are more progressive/left-leaning

PURPLE- Mixed/centrist

United West Coast Federation (UWCF) (California, Western Oregon, Western Washington, Nevada-counties that border California only)-Several counties in eastern Oregon and Washington peacefully broke away and became a part of Idaho. A portion of northern California and southern Oregon have declared their independence and called themselves Jefferson. There is currently a violent insurgency in this area reminiscent of Northern Ireland. The National Guards of California, Western Oregon, and Western Washington have combined. Only the Nevada counties bordering California are within the Federation. UWCF troops are deployed to the area and are conducting counterinsurgency operations.

Texarkana (Texas, Arkansas, Oklahoma)-Arguably the most peaceful section of the former U.S.

United States of the South (USS) (South Carolina, North Carolina, Tennessee, Kentucky, Georgia, Alabama, Mississippi, and Louisiana)-There is a full-blown civil war occurring in Georgia with numerous documented atrocities committed on the Georgia government's behalf. In North Carolina, several insurgent groups operate in urban areas sympathetic to their ideas, mainly Asheville and the Raleigh-Durham area. These groups have been blamed for numerous high-profile bombings, including the bombing at the Memorial Day Coca-Cola 600 NASCAR race that killed 219 attendees and injured over 500 others. They have denied responsibility for any of the bombings.

Don't Tread on Me Upper Midwest Confederation (Illinois, Michigan, Wisconsin, Ohio, Indiana, West Virginia) - Illinois is in a current state of armed conflict, and there are two "declared governments". The divide is mainly between Chicago and its surrounding counties and the rest of Illinois. An influx of support from Ohio and Wisconsin fuels it. Cleveland, Ohio, is still in a state of emergency, but city officials and prominent sports teams are working together to quell the violence.

The Farm Belt Coalition (Iowa, Kansas, Missouri, Nebraska) - A loose confederation of states that have a shared interest in pooling resources to promote their agriculture. Their organization is similar to a less structured EU. Their borders are open to each other, and they have the same trade policies.

**Greater Idaho/New Washington-Idaho, eastern counties in Washington, Oregon, and Nevada. Arguably the most staunchly conservative and militarized former U.S. entity. They maintain a hostile relationship with the U.W.C.F., especially since the eastern parts of Nevada, Oregon, and Washington have broken away from their states and joined them.

The Independent States of the West (ISW)-Colorado, New Mexico, Arizona. These states still maintain some independence and their combined efforts resemble the old Articles of Confederation.

The Mountain Empire-North Dakota, South Dakota, Wyoming, Montana. These former states have declared themselves as an independent country.

Utah (separate)-Utah has gone its way and is an independent country. See the discussion below.

Minnesota (separate)-Minnesota is in talks with the government of Canada about merging or a loose political affiliation such as an EU-style relationship.

-(New) United States of America-Old America-New York, Connecticut, Delaware, Vermont, Rhode Island, Maine, New Jersey, Pennsylvania, Virginia (conflict), Maryland, New Hampshire, New York, Massachusetts, Washington, DC - In the state of Virginia south of the Rappahannock River in Fredericksburg to Front Royal in the western part of the state, there have been some outbreaks of violence from those opposed to the government in Washington, DC. They want to break away and become part of the U.S.S. Parts of northern New York are also experiencing violent incidents.

The Independent State of Florida-Florida declared independence from the United States of the New South after the outbreak of violence in Georgia. They subsequently closed their borders after insurgents from Georgia attempted to smuggle stolen radioactive material into the port of Jacksonville. The material was inadvertently detonated during a controlled detonation by local bomb squads, not realizing it was radioactive due to its shielding. The subsequent spread of radioactive material shut down the port for over a year. Florida still maintains close ties to the USS.

Alaska-Independent. As soon as the dissolution of the U.S. became inevitable and the mass desertions started occurring across the U.S. military and with federal law enforcement entities, Alaska declared independence. They immediately took control of all federal installations, and with the exception of an armed standoff at Ft. Wainwright, their breakaway was peaceful.

Hawaii-Independent.

U.S. Territories (Guam, U.S. Virgin Islands, Puerto Rico, American Samoa, Northern Mariana Islands)-The island territories have become de facto independent countries. The former territories in the Pacific, American Samoa, Guam, and the Northern Mariana Islands have formed a loose coalition to pool their resources and protect their interests. The same has happened with Puerto Rico and the U.S. Virgin Islands.

U.S. interests overseas include military bases, embassies, consulates, etc.

At the time of the collapse of the U.S., many of the overseas U.S. military bases were in disarray and a state of confusion. Some military personnel deserted and stopped obeying orders. A good many also maintained their oath to protect the Constitution and waited in the barracks until their commanding officers gave them instructions. In the countries where the U.S. had a large military presence: Germany, Italy, Japan, Korea, the UK, and Turkey, the host nations basically took control of the bases to prevent internal armed conflict between U.S. military personnel. U.S. Navy ships and submarines had mostly returned to their bases.

Nuclear weapons-The status of nuclear weapons and chain of custody has been a thorny and extremely dangerous issue. As the collapse of the U.S. became imminent, thanks to the foresight of senior officials and scientists within the Department of Defense and Energy, all nuclear weapons in both the continental U.S. and some overseas locations have been consolidated and relocated to military and Department of Energy facilities in the states of Nevada, New Mexico, and Texas due to their experience handling fissile material and the ability to safeguard and safely store them.

This massive secret undertaking included the removal of warheads from ICBMs located in silos in Montana, South Dakota, North Dakota, and Wyoming and the movement of nuclear-tipped Polaris submarine missiles from Navy bases in Georgia and Washington state. Also, in conjunction with the International Atomic Energy Agency (IAEA) and NATO forces, part of the U.S. nuclear arsenal in Europe was transferred to NATO control as a counter to Russian aggression in eastern Europe. The only exception is the very public mutiny of the nuclear-armed submarine, the USS Alabama, whose rogue status went on for almost a year until it was destroyed in a military operation conducted by remnants of the U.S. military and NATO forces.

VIGNETTES

Over the years2025 to 2026, I crisscrossed the former United States of America, interviewing people intimately involved in current events as well as some everyday people. Here are their stories.

(ALEXANDRIA, VA) U.S. ARMY COLONEL GEORGE THOMAS, FORMER U.S. ARMY BATTALION SPECIAL FORCES BATTALION COMMANDER STATIONED IN GERMANY

I was one of the last U.S. service members to leave Europe. When everything went to hell in a handbasket, and you had the Constitutional crisis with the Presidential election and the military mutinies in the States, all battalion commanders and higher U.S. troops in Europe were told to restrict their units to base and place extra guards on all arms rooms, motor pools, and ammunition storage facilities. I spent a lot of time talking to my Soldiers about their oath of office to support and defend the Constitution. It became evident that the end was near when over half the States seceded, and the German government quietly surrounded our bases with police and military units.

I never thought I would see the U.S. military dissolve, but that is exactly what it did once large chunks of the U.S. started seceding. Special Forces is a tight-knit community, so we stayed together longer than most. The biggest question was, when the country you had sworn an oath to no longer existed, where do you place your loyalties? Towards the end, we had some incidents of infighting between guys who had different opinions of what direction the country should have gone in. When I saw that, I knew it was over. When you no longer trust the guys, you are supposed to go to combat with, unit cohesion is gone. It was sad, actually.

Please tell us about the attempt by ISIS to steal nukes in Germany.

I guess this is all public knowledge now and the Department of Defense has cleared me to talk about the attack. When it became evident that the U.S. was falling apart, the Department of Defense and the Department of Energy started retrograding nuclear weapons from our forward bases in Europe back to the U.S. My battalion was tasked with providing security for their return. We had to do this in conjunction with the host nations since they guard the nuclear facilities. As we were overseeing the movement of nuclear weapons out of the storage bunkers in Belgium, we were attacked by what appeared to be Belgium military and police but turned out later to be ISIS. It definitely was an inside job. It started with a suicide bomber attack, which left several of our men dead. The gun battle lasted for well over an hour, and we came close to losing the nuclear weapons. At one moment, the bad guys had control of a nuke. Fortunately, our quick reaction force (QRF) arrived, and we were able to regain control.

I arrived on the Quick Reaction Force helicopter, and we started taking fire as soon as we were over the area. Our guys, the ones left alive, were barricaded in a bunker and surrounded. We couldn't just drop an airstrike and risk spreading radioactive material all over kingdom come. The ISIS fighters fought until the last man, and what made it even more difficult was that they were all wearing Belgian military and police uniforms, and you had actual Belgian military and police in the area. When we finally started searching their bodies. They were all booby-trapped.

It really is sobering to think how close we came to losing a nuclear weapon. We are really just starting to see the severe impact of the loss of the U.S. on the world stage. It isn't very comforting in many ways. Oh well, the world is someone else's problem now. Like China?

What is your current status?

Like a lot of the members of the former military, we are in limbo and either stay where we were based or go back to where we came from or where our loyalties lie. I moved back to the DC area. I grew up as a military brat, so the Army was my home. I report to Ft. Belvoir, VA, on a weekly basis, but it seems a little futile at times, and we are not working. I partly think the government doesn't want a bunch of unemployed, disgruntled, highly-trained former soldiers with nothing to do. We have seen this story before in Iraq in the 2000s.

Did you hear from many of the Soldiers who were in your unit?

Yes, many of them moved to more conservative locations throughout the country, and some went where they thought they could do the best by backing governments abroad and Stateside, or what used to be "Stateside," fighting insurgencies or actually fighting in the insurgencies. Others have joined the militaries of English-speaking countries like Australia, Canada, and the UK.

(ATLANTA, GA) CIVIL RIGHTS LAWYER TURNED MILITIA LEADER

We are using just the first name of Jeff, the leader of the Atlanta militia who is in a fight with the forces of the United States of the South (U.S.S.). To meet him, we first had to change vehicles three times and were blindfolded for most of the trip. They took away my cell phone and only allowed pen and paper for this interview. We were also thoroughly searched every time we stopped.

Jeff, your security measures were fairly drastic. Why is that?

I have had numerous attempts made against my life. The U.S.S. would like to see me eliminated. These precautions are necessary. The U.S.S. has thrown around a lot of money to see me killed. The latest attempt was from my inner circle. Someone that I had known since before all this started. They held out the hope for medical treatment for his mother.

As you know, most of the medical services in Atlanta are nonexistent, especially for a chronic disease. He betrayed me for his mother. Fortunately, I left the room where the explosive was located minutes before the blast. Five other militia members were not so lucky.

Can you discuss the goals of your movement and how you got here?

Well, I was a lawyer arguing civil rights and discrimination cases before the dissolution of the U.S., as well as a pastor. When the Georgia General Assembly voted to secede, it was a slap in the face. Most people in Atlanta wanted to stay a part of the U.S. We have been down this path before, and the result was Atlanta burned to the ground and the continued subjugation of black people.

Also, all of the black legislators in the Georgia House voted against secession. Part of the rallying cry for secession was that Georgia no longer shared the "values" that the U.S. represented. The rationale was more than "our Presidential candidate was not elected." The debate definitely took on some overtly racial undertones. Critical Race Theory and the woke agenda had taken over the country, according to the secessionists. The entire black caucus walked out after the vote.

As soon as the vote became public, protestors took to the streets, and it quickly turned violent. Much of the violence took place in the black areas of Atlanta. We tried to enter talks with the city of Atlanta government, which was very sympathetic towards the protestors and the state government, but after the Oakland City Massacre, all talks ceased, and a full-blown insurgency took place.

As far as our goals, they are to allow Atlanta to go it alone and be a separate entity from the rest of the so-called United States of the South. Our values and beliefs are different from the rest of Georgia and the U.S.S. We are a predominantly black city and have had to suffer gerrymandering and underrepresentation for decades. Why not leave us in peace?

Was your organization involved in the Memorial Day Coca-Cola 600 NASCAR race bombing that killed 219 attendees and injured over 500 others?

We had no involvement with that bombing. While we sympathize with the goals of the alleged bombers, we do not condone violence against innocent civilians (an anonymous post on social media claimed responsibility and said the bombing took place in protest to the U.S.S.'s illegal secession from the U.S. as well as the heavy-handed tactics of the U.S.S. government).

How do you actually see that separation happening? Atlanta is completely isolated from any former state's border or coastline. It could be surrounded like West Berlin during the Cold War, cut off from any allies and always under threat of invasion.

I am not saying it would be easy, but I think in time, we could work things out through rail lines and airports. Right now, it looks like downtown Baghdad in 2006, with barricades and checkpoints everywhere. I just do not see us ever being a part of the U.S.S. There is even serious talk of reviving the Confederate Battle Flag as their flag! I am not sure if it was ignorance or racism. The idea of reviving that flag is beyond disgusting and shows a complete lack of compassion and respect for the black race. I thought we were past that.

(KNOXVILLE, TN, CAPITOL OF THE U.S.S.) LIEUTENANT GENERAL HANK COMBS, COMMANDER, COMBINED ARMED FORCES OF THE UNITED STATES OF THE SOUTH

Tell me about your background, the breakup of the U.S., and the ongoing fight in Georgia.

I was in the U.S. Army for many years as an infantry officer, got out, went to the University of Georgia Law School and joined the Georgia National Guard. I moved up through the officer ranks and eventually was appointed as the Adjutant General for the state of Georgia by Governor Kemp. When the U.S. broke up and the United States of the South was being formed, we decided to consolidate our National Guard forces, and the President appointed me as the Commander of the Combined Forces of the South. The Senate confirmed me, and here I am.

The fight in and around Atlanta is a full-blown insurgency, and unfortunately, it is mainly divided along racial lines. It reminds me of Iraq at the heart of the insurgency. If you are in a military or police vehicle, you will be attacked. All of the government buildings are clustered in areas behind blast walls. There has been talk of abandoning the city, which I support. We lose 20-30 people a day. I say we leave the city, cordon it off, and isolate it.

Can you explain what the insurgents are fighting for?

The insurgents say that the Government of the Southern States of America is illegal and based on racist principles. They say that there should have been a referendum of succession where all citizens voted. My counter is that their duly elected officials in the state legislatures of Georgia, North Carolina, South Carolina, Alabama, Tennessee, Kentucky, Mississippi, West Virginia, Louisiana, and Florida, before they broke off, voted to secede. The U.S. was breaking up, and there was nothing that anyone could do to stop it. The divisions were too great. The last straw for many in the USS was when Kamala Harris became President in what we considered an illegal move. A blind man could have seen it coming. We were too different and the differences became ungovernable. I was stationed in California for many years ago and it felt like a foreign country. You cannot throw a stick in the U.S.S. without hitting a church or a gun store. In California, you cannot throw a stick without hitting a marijuana dispensary and good luck finding a church. For me, a community that does not have a firm foundation in the belief of God is doomed to fail. I don't care who you worship, but you have to believe in something bigger than yourself. Without that basis, what do you have? You have decadence, a self-centeredness that permeates everything you do. I am a Christian and our faith is based on forgiveness and a community of other believers sharing common values.

How do you reconcile your beliefs with the beliefs of the insurgents? Their leader is a former preacher. He is a Christian, too.

Let's just say we agree to disagree. I think his ideas of "inclusivity" go against Christianity. They say they are fighting for freedom and the right to choose. When we first broke away, many communities in Atlanta started rioting and looting their neighborhoods. It was complete chaos. There was absolutely no reason for them to do this. They thought that there was no longer a police force and tried to take advantage of the situation. The Governor declared martial law and sent in National Guard troops to restore order. That is when fighting broke out. Yes, there were several situations, such as the Oakland City incident, that could have been handled better.

Let's talk about the Oakland City Massacre, where 121 black youths were killed. That is considered the starting point for the insurgency and their grievances. They were throwing rocks at about 50 National Guardsmen who were heavily armed. Several shots rang out, and the National Guardsmen opened up with a .50 caliber machine gun. Don't you think that was an extremely disproportionate response?

Also, as a former military officer who swore an oath to defend the U.S. Constitution, how do you reconcile what happened to the U.S. and your current duties?

First, the so-called massacre was not started by Guardsmen. The criminals in the crowd were itching for a fight. The Guardsmen started taking fire from the rooftops of buildings in every direction. They were trapped and were in a fight for their lives. They had no choice but to open fire to save their own lives. Yes, they had a .50 caliber machine gun, but what would you have done? In my humble opinion, once the States started seceding in mass, the United States ceased to exist. I had also taken an oath to support and defend the Constitution of the State of Georgia, so it was a no-brainer.

What about the Georgia National Guardsmen who deserted or who are supporting the insurgency?

This is the ugly part of war. They are considered deserters and can face execution. As reported in the press, we have had to execute several of those who had blood on their hands from killing their former comrades.

What about the other area of the U.S.S. that is experiencing violence, western North Carolina? Do you attribute the bombing at the Memorial Day Coca-Cola 600 in Charlotte, NC, to the group there or the uprising in Atlanta?

The bombing at the NASCAR race was beyond the pale. They killed 219 people and seriously injured over 500 others. These were innocent people just trying to have a good time. There were also numerous children and pregnant women killed.

These groups that claim to be fighting "for the people" killed people they are supposedly helping. Even though they have not claimed responsibility, we have intercepted communications and also a confession from two members that they are responsible. We are also seeing collaboration between the group in Atlanta and the group in western North Carolina. They are murderers, and I promise to bring them to swift justice.

How do you answer the complaints of heavy-handed tactics used by your forces across the U.S.S.? The complaints include targeting people of color at vehicle checkpoints and border crossings, illegal detentions for indefinite periods, "night raids", and torture of people in your custody.

First, everything we do is in accordance with the rule of law. The President of the U.S.S. reluctantly declared martial law due to the unprecedented levels of violence. The responsibility of every government is the protection of its people. That is one basic responsibility that the old U.S. government failed to do. We will not make the same mistake. Martial law gives duly authorized security forces, such as the National Guard and police, the power to detain and question people for up to 48 hours without bringing charges against them. Our officers are taught only to detain when they have a reasonable suspicion backed up by their actions, evidence, or behavior that the person being detained is conducting illegal activities. We do not target people of color. We do, though, have a suspect profiling program that has been very effective.

As far as the charge of torture, our official policy is no torture. I do acknowledge that we have had some isolated incidents of aggressive behavior during interviews, and we immediately disciplined those involved.

Can you provide more details on this program? What are some of the profiling criteria?

The details of that program are classified so we do not give our adversaries information that they could use to counter our efforts.

(SACRAMENTO, CA, CAPITOL OF THE U.W.C.F.) FORMER U.S. CONGRESSWOMAN LANEY STEEDMAN, LOS ANGELES/CURRENT MEMBER OF THE WEST COAST FEDERATION LEGISLATURE

Congresswoman Steedman, thank you for speaking with us. As a former member of the U.S. Congress who was intimately involved during the turmoil of the post-2024 election, you have an insider's perspective of the events that led up to the collapse of the U.S. Can you explain what exactly happened? It wasn't very clear for many people since it involved aspects of the U.S. Constitution that had rarely been invoked before.

Those definitely were some confusing and heartbreaking times. We all had to become Constitutional scholars to be able to legislate effectively. Everything was made more difficult with all of the misinformation. When there was no clear winner of the majority of electoral college votes (the winner has to have at least 270 electoral college votes), according to the U.S. Constitution, the decision was then in the hands of Congress according to the 12th and 20th Amendments. The vote for the Presidency is the responsibility of the House of Representatives, and the vote for the Vice President is in the Senate. The House vote requires a simple majority, BUT it is not "one Congressman equals one vote." Each state's Congressional House delegation is allowed one vote, and within each state's delegation, if they cannot reach a majority decision, their vote is split and does not count. There is no limit on the number of votes that can take place. The only limit is the decision must be made by January 20 according to the 20th Amendment. If the House cannot decide by then, then the Vice President-elect shall "act" as the President. Here is where things got tricky.

According to the 12th Amendment, the Senate must vote a simple majority for Vice President, and it is one vote per Senator. If the Senate cannot decide by January 20 on a Vice President, then according to the 20th Amendment, "the Congress may by law provide for the case wherein neither a President-elect nor a Vice President-elect shall have qualified, declaring who shall then act as President, or the manner in which one who is to act shall be selected, and such person shall act accordingly until a President or Vice President shall be qualified." Also "if a President shall not have been chosen before the time fixed for the beginning of his term, or if the President-elect shall have failed to qualify, then the Vice President-elect shall act as President until a President shall have qualified." Neither the Constitution nor the Amendments explain how "a President shall have qualified." The House was not able to decide on a President by January 20, 2025, and as a result, Vice President-elect Harris, whom the Senate elected, became acting President. This situation has never happened in the history of the U.S. Of course, there were court challenges and the Supreme Court refused to rule on the case, which effectively was a tacit ruling which validated Vice President-elect Harris as the acting President. Then, you had the subsequent terrorist attack on the Court. The ambiguity of the decision, coupled with the poisonous, polarized atmosphere, expedited the collapse of the U.S. All sides felt like they had been wronged and that their candidate was the lawfully elected President.

Then you had the conflicting lower Court rulings about the legality of Harris' election and the subsequent succession of Idaho.

What was happening in Congress during this period? And what were some of the proposals?

It was chaos. Debates started on how to select a permanent President which immediately descended into shouting matches with several House delegations walking out. Some of the House wanted to continue voting until a President was elected. Others wanted to enact a Constitutional amendment to clarify the subsequent Presidential election process and then a loud minority wanted to have another Constitutional convention to redo the Constitution completely. It reached a point where all decorum and House rules went by the wayside. Once we no longer had a quorum of Representatives due to the walkouts, the House could no longer legislate, and with the state secessions, Congress ceased to exist. It was both surreal and tragic.

What happened to you personally when this occurred?

Well, I packed up my essential personal belongings from my apartment and left for California. It took me several days to get home since the DC airports were jammed and the airlines were in chaos. The federal government runs our air traffic control system, and once you no longer had a "head" the "body" of air traffic controllers started falling apart.

When I made it back to California over the subsequent year, the United West Coast Federation (UWCF) formed, consisting of California, Western Oregon, Western Washington, and Nevada counties bordering California-counties that border California. It was decided to establish an interim legislature consisting of duly elected former US. Congressmen. It has been a lot of work starting a new government, but it has also been very rewarding. We are really trying to learn from the mistakes of the U.S. as well as fix the problems within the California state legislature. We now have a constitution that is very similar to the original U.S. Constitution but without misogyny and the 2nd Amendment! I am proud of the work we have done.

(UNDISCLOSED LOCATION, WESTERN NORTH CAROLINA) "SCOTT", LEADER OF THE ASHEVILLE RESISTANCE

***The meeting with the leader of the Asheville Resistance (AR) leader took place in a secret location and changed vehicles multiple times, blindfolded.*

What is your background?

I actually was a kayaking instructor and an outdoor skills teacher. I was also a former U.S. Army infantry officer. The skills have actually come in handy being part of the resistance in a mountainous environment. I know these mountains like the back of my hand and many of the soldiers in the AR are outdoorsmen, so we are able to operate freely here.

Can you tell me how the AR was formed and its goals?

When the breakup of the U.S. happened, it really shook me to my core. I consider myself an American patriot and believe in the ideals of the U.S. freedom of speech, the right to live your own life as you choose, and the protection of the most vulnerable segments of our population. When the government in Raleigh started to pass these draconian laws that limited the right to assemble and criminalize homosexuality, I had to act. My brother is a gay man and the most decent human being that I have ever known. I tried to lobby the legislature and when that didn't work, I started the protests. After multiple arrests for just peacefully protesting, I knew peaceful means would not work. In jail, I was severely beaten by the police and tortured. I left jail with a determination to right these wrongs. I believe enough in this cause to die for it. The Asheville community has many like-minded individuals, and we started organizing. Our initial plans were to start with educating the people about the wrongs of the Raleigh government through hacking government sites and "midnight letters" to the homes of the leaders of the legislature. When that didn't work, we resorted to violent means. Initially, our goals were to overturn the legislation and go back to core American values. Now we realize that our differences are so great. The Asheville area just needs to break away and form its government. We are in coordination with the resistance in Atlanta as well.

Was the AR involved in the Memorial Day Coca-Cola 600 NASCAR race bombing that killed 219 attendees and injured over 500 others?

We had no involvement with that bombing. I agree with the goals of those behind the bombing, but definitely not the means. The killing of innocent men, women, and children goes against our code of conduct, is abhorrent, and all it does is drive people to turn away from our cause (an anonymous post on social media claimed responsibility and said the bombing took place in protest to the U.S.S.'s illegal secession from the U.S. as well as the heavy-handed tactics of the U.S.S. government).

Can you tell me what life is like now for you and your organization?

It has not been an easy life. We are under constant threat from the authorities, and we have to move often. Plus, we have to deal with collaborators in our midst. The police will arrest our members, then torture them and threaten their families if they do not cooperate with them. The tragic part of this is that I knew many of the law enforcement officers in my community before everything fell apart. I taught them, drank beer with them and kayaked with them. It just goes to show you that even decent people are capable of doing horrible things. I am thankful that I do not have kids. My wife is a doctor, and when the country started breaking down, the medical system started falling apart, too. Our entire system is based on the insurance companies which operate nationally. They were not set up to work as individual entities in different states. People would come into the hospital thinking that their insurance would cover them but was told they had to pay out of pocket since the insurance companies were no longer working. There is actually a barter system now for medical care.

Can you tell me more about this barter system?

- Scott's wife, the doctor, enters the room.

Hi, Marie (a pseudonym) thank you for talking with me. Can you tell me about how medical care works now?

Well, a patient will come into the hospital, and since the entire medical insurance system collapsed, the first thing that is discussed is payment. We will take anything in kind. Farmers are the easiest.

They will bring in produce, meat, etc., with the promise of regular payments. Others will provide services like an electrician or a carpenter. The most valuable skills are those who can fix computers and telephones. The entire U.S. supply chain has broken down. In the U.S., we were always used to having something break and just going to buy a new phone or whatever. That doesn't happen anymore. You have to fix it.

Do you still accept cash or credit cards?

Cash is iffy. I am not an economics guru, but I do know the U.S. dollar was completely based on faith in the stability of the U.S. government. Some people still trust the dollar; others do not. I know that the credit card companies are in talks with the mini-states to develop bilateral agreements so it really depends upon where you live and if an agreement is in place.

What about the quality of healthcare? How has that been affected?

The skills of doctors and nurses have not degraded, but as I said, the supply chain has been disrupted. We have severe shortages of everything, especially essential medications and antibiotics. Antibiotic shortages and research were already a problem before the collapse. China is the main manufacturer and the only U.S. company that makes the primarily used antibiotics is in Briston, Tennessee.[8] They have reduced their manufacturing, and with the cost of shipping skyrocketing the prices have gone up dramatically with the supply shortages. One note on the skills of doctors: we are required to receive continuing education, and a lot of that involves traveling to other states. Right now, that whole system is in limbo and not really working so the improvement of the skills of doctors exchanging best practices across the states is not happening. So yes, medical skills will start to stagnate. At the end of the day, though, I only know of a handful of hospitals that are turning away patients. We still follow the Hippocratic Oath.

---

[8] Press Release PR Newswire, "US Antibiotics, the Nation's Sole Amoxicillin Manufacturing Facility, Launches Production to Secure Critical Supply Chain," *Business Insider*, November 30, 2021, https://markets.businessinsider.com/news/stocks/usantibiotics-the-nation-s-sole-amoxicillin-manufacturing-facility-launches-production-to-secure-critical-supply-chain-1031012615#:~:text=USAntibiotics%20is%20the%20only%20U.S.%20manufacturer%20of%20amoxicillin,widely%20available%20for%20the%20benefit%20of%20all%20Americans.

(CHICAGO, ILLINOIS) MAYOR RAHM EMANUEL OF CHICAGO

The interview with the mayor of Chicago was repeatedly interrupted by gunfire and explosives. Mayor Emanuel, thank you for taking the time to talk with us.

Can you tell us a little background on how you ended up as a mayor of Chicago again?

"Yes, when the U.S. started to collapse, I was the U.S. ambassador to Japan. I saw Chicago in turmoil and basically leaderless after the previous mayor was assassinated. The trip back was quite a journey trying to get back into Chicago. The state government has declared Chicago in open rebellion and shut down the two major airports here. I flew into Detroit, Michigan, and was detained for two days thereby Michigan State Troopers based on an Illinois warrant. Completely trumped-up charges. Then I traveled across the peninsula to Lake Michigan and then took a boat to Chicago. I had to be smuggled across "the border" into Chicago, basically. The city council was in turmoil, and in an emergency session, they voted me as the interim mayor.

What is the situation now in Chicago and the surrounding area?

Well, we are in open conflict between the city of Chicago and the "state" of Illinois. The Illinois government says that Chicago is part of Illinois and does not have a right to be a separate entity. The problem in Chicago was when the U.S. started to dissolve and the Illinois legislature decided to go it on their own, parts of Chicago started to riot and loot. It was too much for the police to handle, and so the National Guard was called in. The violence escalated, and we had several unjustified shootings of protesters similar to what you have seen in Atlanta. Also, there is a racial element to all of this. Much of the white population left the city once the violence started, so now you have a case of mostly blacks fighting against the National Guard. I protested to the Illinois governor to pull back the Guard and try and give some breathing space, but he sent in more troops. Several of the Guard units located in Chicago either refused to participate or joined the protesters and here we are today. The Guard units loyal to the state of Illinois have pulled out of the city and have instituted a blockade while the Guardsmen loyal to the city, sit on the other side facing them. The blockade is very porous, given Lake Michigan and the major gaps in the lines, but fighting takes place every day. Our electricity and basic services are severely degraded, and food and safe water are becoming scarce.

So, is there a peaceful way out of this?

Right now, I do not see a peaceful way out. Tensions and rhetoric are too high, and blood has already been spilled. I think the best we can hope for right now is a stalemate.

How can you hold out longer without external support?

Well, we are receiving support from the UN and the Red Cross and from some other governments that I am not at liberty to reveal (Mayor Emanuel is referring to clandestine support coming from Canada and California). We are able to hold out for quite a while. I will not say indefinitely, but we can survive. Chicagoans are used to harsh conditions. Just look at our winters and the amount of gun violence this city has been through.

What are your ultimate goals?

We want to be left to our own devices to establish our separate political entity or city-state. Historically, there has always been this friction between Chicago and the rest of the state of Illinois. This is a chance for us to go our separate ways. As I mentioned before, there is a racial element to this as well. I am not advocating segregation, but I am advocating letting Chicagoans govern Chicagoans.

What was the Japanese perspective of what was going on in the U.S.?

They were in disbelief. The Japanese are one of our staunchest allies, and the U.S. rebuilt their entire form of government and country after World War II. Their Constitution was written by U.S. General Douglas MacArthur, for Christ's sake!

The dissolution of the U.S. has brought about a lot of insecurity and uncertainty in Japan. Our nuclear umbrella protected them, and they counted on us to counter Chinese and North Korean aggression. They are actually seriously debating developing their nuclear weapons in the Diet, their legislative body.

I had a lot of government and private Japanese citizens express sympathy for our plight. The situation in the U.S. has really shaken them to their core. America was always seen as permanent and unwavering.

What are your personal views on the dissolution of the U.S.?

I consider it a tragedy, and we cannot even begin to fathom the unforeseen negative consequences of its breakup both here in the U.S. and around the world. The world just became a much more dangerous place, and the threat of nuclear is the greatest it has been since the Cuban Missile Crisis. Be careful what you ask for…

(MIAMI, FL, UNIVERSITY OF MIAMI CAMPUS) PROFESSOR MICHAEL CAPERS, POLITICAL SCIENCE PROFESSOR, UNIVERSITY OF MIAMI

Professor Capers, thank you for taking the time to talk with me during these trying times. I will just jump right into it.

Did you see the break-up of the U.S. coming, and how did events transpire in Florida?

Academically, I saw the breakup coming with the widening divisions in the country during the 2010s without even a remote possibility of reconciliation, but emotionally, I didn't think it would happen. Heck, I worked at the U.S. State Department for ten years, implementing U.S. foreign policy. I completely bought into American exceptionalism.

In Florida, when the other Southern states seceded and formed the United States of the South (USS), Florida enthusiastically joined. There is strength in numbers, especially of like-minded people. Unfortunately, we were quickly caught up in the violence just across the border in Georgia. Since the release of radioactive materials happened at the port of Jacksonville, Governor Desantis immediately shut our borders down with Georgia and Alabama. Soon afterward, the governors of Alabama and Georgia issued threatening statements against the closure and pushed National Guard troops to our border. The Florida Legislature voted to secede from the USS for our security. We are since on amenable terms with the USS, but we are just fine going it on our own.

What makes Florida different from other former states?

We are politically cohesive. We have a large conservative population comprised of evangelical Christians, Jews, and Hispanics from across the Caribbean and South America. We just want stability and the ability to do things our way. The identity politics of the early 2020s were not very popular here. The emergence of a potentially progressive federal administration was the final straw for a lot of Floridians. We have been experiencing a 'decades-long migration from folks in the northeast moving here due to the weather, cost of living, and politics. Floridians still believe in the original idea of America, but it has diverged to the point that we can no longer recognize large parts of America as part of a shared consciousness. I am personally sad to see the U.S. break apart, but it had become ungovernable, and the Constitution was too ambiguous, so ideas, concepts, and norms could easily be controlled and manipulated by vocal minorities. I know that concerns are cut both ways with "red" and "blue" states. Now, that doesn't really matter much, does it?

How has the breakup affected the economy?

Florida, like the rest of the former U.S., sunk into a recession but was fortunate enough not to fall into the "unspoken" depression like in some other places throughout the South. It has been left unsaid, but one of the many reasons Florida struck out on its own is we didn't want to have to pay to bail out other States that were in dire straits. We were struggling just to keep our economy afloat. We are having to assume the responsibilities of the federal government on a scale never imagined to include trade deals with other former entities of the U.S. as well as foreign governments. We are fortunate that we have the coastline and port facilities that we do. Also, we have a large presence in the aerospace industry with Cape Canaveral, and our biomedical industry is world-class.[9] Florida is still a major tourist destination, and we have seen our population almost double since the collapse of the U.S.

Historically, do you think the breakup was inevitable? You mentioned the ambiguity in the Constitution.

Well, the end state of all empires is the decline and eventual collapse. Why would we be different?

However, the world had never seen an empire like the U.S., a benevolent (at times) and reluctant empire. It always seemed like we were in a perpetual identity crisis with who we were as a people and our role in the world.

I do not fault the Founders of the U.S. for the system that they came up with. I do not think anyone else could have done better, and they were some of the greatest and most learned minds of the time. I just do not think a country this size with so much diversity is governable within a democracy.

---

[9] "Life Sciences," Select Florida, accessed on May 1, 2024, https://selectflorida.org/why-florida/industries/life-sciences/

Look, I am not autocratic, and I believe in democracy, but democracy is messy and inefficient. It was initially designed for direct citizen participation, but a country the size of the U.S. cannot realistically do that; that is why we, our founders, chose a republican, little "R" form of government. Take a look at Russia with its size and diverse population. Since the time of the czars, it has taken an authoritarian government to run the place. Again, I am not advocating dictatorships, but is democracy the best system of government for a country this size? Maybe some sort of hybrid.

Just take a look at the various mini-states that now comprise the former U.S. Some of them definitely have an authoritarian slant, like the USS. When citizens do not feel safe, they will choose security over freedom almost any day. That is part of the reason, I think, that the U.S. collapsed. Many parts of America felt unsafe, underrepresented, and ignored, and their governments now reflect that. You can see that one of the results of the breakup was the "great migration" where Americans moved to the enclaves that most closely represent their values. The two political entities that have seen the most population growth is the USS and UWCF, the most conservative and most liberal countries. Utah is an interesting case study as well. They chose to go it alone and stick with their tribe. I do not count the outliers like Alaska or Hawaii. Geographically, it just made sense for them to go it alone. According to the last U.S. census, ever, in 2020 over 60% of Utahns are members of The Church of Jesus Christ of Latter-day Saints.[10] Utah is also the most stable mini-state in existence now. You would have expected them to become more of a theocracy or lean towards authoritarianism, with the Church having a stranglehold on power. The opposite is true. They are one of the more "open societies" amongst all the political entities that comprise the former U.S. Alcohol has not been banned, and abortions, while restricted, are allowed under certain circumstances. Same-sex marriage is enshrined in their constitution. My analysis is that they are comfortable in their skin, and much of their population shares the same values and beliefs. They do not feel threatened or feel a need to restrict behavior that goes against their personal beliefs.

[10] [10] Jonathon Sharp, "Utah is no longer majority Mormon, new research says," *ABC4.com*, December 29, 2023, https://www.abc4.com/news/wasatch-front/utah-is-no-longer-majority-mormon-new-research-says/.

(VIENNA, AUSTRIA, NEW UN HEADQUARTERS) UNDERSECRETARY OF THE UN HANS FRIDOR

I want to thank Undersecretary Hans Fridor for taking the time out of his busy schedule, which includes the gargantuan task of moving the UN headquarters from New York City to Vienna, Austria.

Can you explain with the limited time that you have what has happened throughout the world as a result of the collapse of the U.S.?

The disintegration of the U.S. has had a severe cascading effect around the world. They really were the world's policeman, no matter how reluctant they were and no matter how their adversaries wished they were not. The world has become a more dangerous place since it collapsed. Just take a tour around the world:

-Iran and Israel have been in open conflict for six months now without an arbitrator or someone standing between them. Ever since the October 2023 Hamas attack, conflict in the Middle East has escalated dramatically. The continuous attacks on shipping and the withdrawal of the U.S. Navy from the world's oceans is like someone has declared open season on shipping. Most shipping is now diverted around the Horn of Africa, greatly increasing the worldwide cost of everything from oil to food. Iran tested its first nuclear weapons six months ago, about the time that the war started between Iran and Israel. It is the first war between two nuclear-armed countries since India and Pakistan.

-Without the nuclear umbrella and tacit security agreements between the U.S. and Saudi Arabia, it has started a nuclear weapons program of its own as well as Australia and South Korea. We also suspect several other countries are following suit, including Brazil, Egypt, Jordan, Poland, and the UAE. Even Japan is considering starting its programs.

-Eastern Europe has become the fiefdom of Russia. NATO is still in existence, but it is just a paper tiger without the U.S. Emboldened by the collapse of the U.S., Russia permanently annexed the Ukrainian lands they took in 2014 and 2022, and after all U.S. support for Ukraine ceased, Ukraine continued the fight admirably with support from the UK and other European states, but with the split in Europe brought on by the lack of U.S. leadership and advanced weapons, most aid stopped.

Ukraine had to sue for peace under favorable conditions for Russia. They lost all the lands previously annexed to include Donbas and Crimea. They also promised not to join the EU and NATO and vowed a neutral foreign policy. The Zelensky government was voted out, and now you have a government in power that is more amenable to the Russians. Russia has basically annexed Belarus, Georgia, and Moldova. The three Baltic states are basically isolated, cut off, and dare not cross Russia. The only reason Russia has not moved into NATO countries is because they still possess nuclear weapons, and Article V, an attack on one is an attack on all, is still in effect. Russia has followed its standard playbook and disrupted Europe with disinformation and the fomenting of dissent. In almost every country, Russia has said there is some form of repression against Slavic people, and with their controversial automatic Russian citizenship for all "oppressed" Slavs, it has given them cover to "assist" those Slavs.

Europe has become a massive armed continent. There are two camps in Europe now. Those who oppose Russia and those who appease or ally themselves with them. It is interesting to see that the countries that suffered the most under Communism are the strongest opponents of Russia. Poland has become an armed autocratic state, and it is an open secret that they have started their own nuclear weapons program. The UK has basically removed itself from European affairs. It is trying to fill some of the void with the U.S.'s withdrawal from policing the world's oceans and Middle Eastern hotspots, but they just do not have the capacity. France has tried to fill the leadership void in Europe, but with the election of a far-right government, they are more sympathetic to Russia. Germany has all but ceded leadership and declared that it will fulfill its NATO treaty responsibilities, but its actions show appeasement towards Russia. They have restarted the oil pipeline that was stopped at the start of the Russian 2022 attack against Ukraine. The pro-Russia camp includes the usual suspects. They are just more open about it: Hungary, Serbia, and Slovakia. The bright spot is that the Nordic states, Denmark, Finland, Norway, and Sweden, have really stepped up their leadership and military muscle. They are more and more pooling their economic and military might to form a strong bloc in Europe. Their combined strengths serve as a strong counter to Russia and are keeping Russia in check. Right now, Europe is in its most volatile state since right before the beginning of World War II.

- The terrorist group ISIS has been making a comeback in Syria and western Iraq. Russia has been sending more troops into Syria to stop their resurgence, and the UK and France have tried to fill the void in western Iraq.
- North Korea has increased its saber-rattling, with war looking imminent at times on the Peninsula. The disintegration and withdrawal of U.S. troops in South Korea has removed any checks on North Korean aggression. It has been revealed that South Korea is pursuing a nuclear weapon program of its own.
- Since the U.S. stopped patrolling the Pacific and, specifically, the South China Sea, China has defacto control of all the disputed islands and controls all shipping in the area. There has also been a major realignment of loyalties in the Pacific, with China and most of the smaller countries on one side and Australia, India, Japan, New Zealand, and South Korea on the other. There is talk of a NATO like organization being established between those countries, but without a superpower to anchor an alliance, it will not have much teeth. As mentioned before, Australia and South Korea have reportedly started pursuing their own nuclear weapons programs, with Japan possibly following their lead.

Taiwan

The government of Taiwan sees the writing on the wall and is in negotiations with mainland China for closer integration, similar to what took place in Hong Kong. The People's Liberation Army (PLA) operates unchecked in Taiwanese sea and airspace.

South America, which had always been a part of the U.S.'s sphere of influence ever since the declaration of the Monroe Doctrine, has fallen more and more under the sway of China. Brazil and Venezuela are emerging as the major power players in the region. Brazil has reportedly restarted its nuclear weapons program. Immigration is still a problem along the former U.S.'s southern border. China now has a military base in Venezuela.

The continent of Africa is becoming more and more tied to China. With the withdrawal of the U.S. from Africa, China has filled the void with its Belt & Road Initiative and now has large military bases in Algeria and Dijoubti that include both ground and naval forces.

You have painted a pretty bleak picture. What is your prediction for the future?

Unfortunately, I do not have a very positive outlook at least for the foreseeable future. Nuclear weapons are increasingly everywhere. Every continent but Africa now has nuclear weapons. Whenever there is a proliferation of a new type of weapon, governments tend to choose what to use. Also, since the memories of Hiroshima and Nagasaki are fading, I think the chances of nuclear weapons use have greatly increased. How safe do you think the world is?

Despite all of its flaws, the world needed the U.S. They were the world's reluctant big brother. I do not see China stepping up to ensure the global common seaways are open or naked aggression is checked.

My only hope is that a balance of power will take place. Power hates a vacuum and throughout history, one dominant power never lasts. It is just right now I cannot see a clear path to the checks and balances that competing centers of power brought.

What has happened to the world economy?

Throughout the world, economies have fallen into recession, with the Global South the most affected. Nobody likes to use the "D" word, depression, but some countries are already there. The dollar, which was the currency of choice for decades, is being replaced by the Euro and the Chinese Yuan. So much of the financial system is based on trust in the system, and we are seeing that that confidence has eroded severely.

Has the role of the UN changed at all?

Considering that 22% of our budget came from the U.S., our reach and effectiveness with programs like the World Food Program and UNHCR have dramatically decreased.[11] On the plus side, it looks like we will significantly reform the composition of the UN Security Council so that voting will be more equitable. The non-permanent member's votes will be binding just like the permanent members.

---

[11] CFR.org editors, "Funding the United Nations: How Much Does the U.S. Pay?" *Council on Foreign Relations,* February 29, 2004, Funding the United Nations: How Much Does the U.S. Pay? | Council on Foreign Relations (cfr.org).

Any further comments?

I guess that you will start to see more regional power blocs arising, such as you are witnessing with the Nordic countries in Europe and Australia, India, Japan, New Zealand and South Korea. In the countries that now comprise the former U.S., the current/former U.S. still has some of the elements and instruments of power, and the UWCF has a lot of economic power as well. They both seem to be in alliance as a bulwark against authoritarianism. Much of the U.S. military might have been dispersed to the former states where they were originally based.

(UNDISCLOSED LOCATION, NORTHERN CALIFORNIA) MIKE ROGERS, FORMER NFL PLAYER & CURRENT LEADER OF THE COUNTRY OF JEFFERSON (FORMERLY NORTHERN CALIFORNIA AND SOUTHERN OREGON)

Mr. Rogers, thank you for taking the time to talk with me.

Can you explain what happened in Jefferson and the current situation?

Thank you for your effort to try and explain what happened to the U.S. Historians will be retelling this story for centuries. The state of Jefferson has been an idea that this section of northern California and southern Oregon has been pressing for years. Our politics here are definitely different from those of the rest of California and Oregon. We like to say that our political lineage goes back to the Founding Fathers and the spirit of the precursor to the Founding Fathers, the Sons of Liberty led by Samuel Adams. He did not just have a beer named after him! We believe in individual rights, and the U.S. government's encroachment into personal freedoms during the 2010s was really the straw that broke the camel's back. This was definitely Trump's country. For all of his faults, he spoke the truth to us. As Dave Chapelle aptly said, Trump is a "truthful liar." The woke culture and the troubles on the U.S.-Mexico border showed that we had lost our way as a country where the majority rules. The minority became the rulers and we could just not stand for it. As soon as that traitor, Harris, became president, we seceded.

We have established our own country to include going back to the gold standard for currency. Our currency, the Jeffersonian dollar, is solid and backed by an actual gold reserve. We are in an ongoing conflict with National Guard units from Oregon and Washington, but our citizenry is armed to the teeth, and we are holding our own despite being surrounded. We have time and geography on our side. Most of our country is rugged and mountainous, and the enemy sticks to the roads. Fortunately, we have a lot of retired U.S. military special operations personnel who got us quickly organized and have made it very painful for attacking forces. Also, a lot of area borders sympathetic counties just inside of Nevada.

How do you see this playing out?

As I said, we have time and terrain on our side. Oregon and California have enough problems as it is so they will soon tire of this and let us go our own way. We have the will of our people, which they don't have. It is just a matter of how bloody they want to get.

How did you go from NFL player to leader of a breakaway country in the former U.S.?

(Mike chuckles). Well, I was born and raised in this part of California and my father was really big into the Jefferson movement. Back then it was seen by most as a joke and fringe, but anyone from here will tell that it was serious. When you entered Jefferson, it was identified with signs, and we even had a shadow government ready to take over. Even though back then it was mainly middle-aged men drinking beer and complaining about the government.

I did not pay much attention to it growing up; I was too focused on football, but it obviously influenced me. I played in the NFL for five years. Go Cowboys! Until an injury side-lined. I came back home and tried to open a small business that helped folks recover from injuries using a combination of rehabilitation, sports, and microdoses of marijuana. The focus was on being all natural and staying away from steroids and opioids, and I was shocked at the sheer amount of red tape that included multiple licenses and certifications and then the taxes. Wow. I majored in physical therapy in college, and with my NFL experience, I know just a little bit about what it takes to recover from injuries.

I was trying to help people, but I felt like the government in Sacramento was more interested in preventing folks from opening up businesses. And do not get me started on the federal government and marijuana. The banking issues alone will deter most people. I tried to petition the state legislature for change for over a year to no avail. I always considered myself a proud American and Californian, but every man has his limits. I stopped my efforts and returned to Jefferson with the realization that the California and U.S. governments were so dysfunctional that they were beyond repair. My return coincided with the start of the 2024 election season. I started campaigning for Jefferson to become its state initially, but according to the U.S. Constitution, you cannot break up a state and make it into a new one without the consent of the state's legislature, and that was not going to happen. [12]

Once the writing was on the wall and Idaho seceded, that was our opportunity to go our way. We declared our independence in a referendum vote with over 85% of the population in support, and

[12] Alexa Brock, "Verify: Can states legally be split?" KREM2 News, January 24, 2019, https://www.krem.com/article/news/local/verify-can-states-legally-be-split/293-0bf30eaa-cf31-4d02-a357-60abcbcb9c80

here we are today. We just want to be left alone. Our philosophy is very much what I call conservative libertarianism. It took the state governments in Sacramento and Portland a while to get organized against our secession, but that was to our advantage. We were very well prepared. Like I said, a lot of former Green Berets live here and they quickly got us trained and organized. We knew that we could not take the National Guard head-to-head, so we worked on guerilla tactics. The National Guard is scared to get off of the main roads or get out of their vehicles. They might control the main roads, but that is about it. We have our own cyber and drone army, and we own the air. After we took down several helicopters with swarm drone attacks, they stopped flying here. I think it is just a matter of time, before they just leave us alone. We are making it very painful for them!

(COLUMBIA, SC-SOUTH CAROLINA SENATE) STATE SENATOR JOHN GRAMBLING, PEACH FARMER & STATE SENATOR

Senator John Grambling, thanks for taking the time to talk with me.

As South Carolina was the first state to secede in 1861, it is interesting to get your perspective on the current situation.

When South Carolina seceded, I had my reservations. I come from a family whose lineage proudly stretches back to the Civil War. It seemed like we had done this before, and the first time didn't work out so well. This time around, we were not the first and it seems different with most of the states seceding. Also, the first time around, it was about slavery. Obviously, this time is different.

So why did South Carolina secede? And I know it is academic now. Was it legal? I thought the issue of secession was decided in 1865.

Yeah, it is water under the bridge now. Still, over the past few years prior to the breakup, especially under the Biden administration, it seemed the federal government was acting more and more like the states. The citizens' voices didn't matter. You can take a look at the border crisis. You had the Texas Governor refuse a federal court order to take down border fencing because his state was under assault. Many Republican governors supported his refusal and sent National Guard troops to the Texas border. I was in the Guard at the time and helped push out South Carolina's contribution.

And yes, it looked like the "right" to secede had already been decided. That is one of the reasons that South Carolina was hesitant about seceding. Like I said, things were different this time. We had most of the country ready to leave in some shape, form or fashion, and it was not about human enslavement. In addition, prior to the Civil War, the South was mostly an agrarian country with very little industry. That obviously has changed, so if there were going to be a fight, we would be more easily matched.

Was it legal?

The victors write history, and so by our actions, it was legal. In my view, the federal government had stopped doing its Constitutional duties. They could not even protect our borders. The defense is our nation's job number one for any government, and in that, they were failing. In addition, the election of Harris to the presidency was downright unconstitutional. We had multiple federal courts rule on this.

The Supreme Court refused to rule on it, and two lower federal courts said that her election was in accordance with the Constitution.

True, but like I said, two courts said it wasn't.

What about the oath you swore as an officer to support and defend the Constitution? You were still in the National Guard at the time, right?

Yeah, a lot of us wrestled with the morality of it. As a matter of fact, we had the faculty from the University of South Carolina Law School, as well constitutional law professors from my alma mater, The Citadel, The Military College of South Carolina, speak with all South Carolina National Guard officers. It was unprecedented. We held a weeklong conference about it. You did not see anything like that in South Carolina prior to the Civil War. But what happens if the government that you are sworn to defend fails?

What are the major repercussions of the collapse of the U.S. in South Carolina?

The biggest repercussion for us has been the huge economic downturn coupled with the drought. With the loss of federal insurance, I am about to declare bankruptcy. The supply distribution chain was completely turned on its head with some of the main folks we supply in the Northeast raising tariffs for our products. Plus, the terrorist attacks in Georgia and Florida have disrupted rail lines, so our produce peaches will rot in the summer heat. Yeah, global warming is real.

No offense, but you do not sound like a typical Southern politician with your talk of global warming.

(He laughs) If you want to know what is really going on in the world, talk to a farmer! We live or die by the land.

Thank you for taking the time to talk with me.

Any final words?

Yes, a lot of folks on the left, I guess that distinction does not really matter anymore, blamed Trump for the collapse. Look, Trump did not cause the U.S. to dissolve. It was already on the path. He just was a voice for a lot of Americans like my constituents who felt like they were being blamed for all the world's problems. Do you know the only group of folks that the "woke police" allowed you to make fun of in 2024? Middle-aged white, Southern men. It was perfectly fine to call us backward and slow. Remember what Obama said about how "they" cling to their "guns or religion."[13] Do you know how insulting that was? I grew up going to church every Sunday, saying grace before each meal and praying at night. I also grew up going hunting with my grandfather and father. Shoot, I took hunter safety classes in middle school! Trump was like us. All the elites made fun of his talk, mannerisms and the way he looked. He pushed back and never took any shit. Keep in mind that if he had not stepped up, eventually, someone else would have. Look at the Trump clones around the world. Trump was coming no matter what! Give the guy a break.

[13] Ben Smith, "Obama on small-town Pa.: Clinging to religion, guns, xenophobia," *Politico*, April 11, 2008, https://www.politico.com/blogs/ben-smith/2008/04/obama-on-small-town-pa-clinging-to-religion-guns-xenophobia-007737

(SIOUX FALLS, SD) REVEREND ED MASTERSON, FOUNDER & HEAD PASTOR FOR THE CHURCH OF HOPE

Reverend Masterson, thanks for taking the time to talk with us. You have one of the largest and most influential evangelical Christian churches in the U.S. As such, you have a finger on the spiritual pulse of a lot of Americans. The evangelical Christian movement really embraced the Republican MAGA movement, and some people blame your support for adding fuel to the secession fire and giving folks the religious cover to support the dissolution of the U.S. I know from personal experience that amongst some Christians, there was almost a giddiness or excitement that the "end days" or a Revelation type event was happening. How do you respond to that, and overall, what does Christianity have to say about the events in the U.S. over the past few years?

Well, first, I take offense that Christians were happy to see the U.S. dissolve. I always considered myself a Christian first and a proud American second. My congregation was always staunchly patriotic. I would argue that their love of America and the degradation of the values that made our country great caused many of them to see breaking up the country as the only way to get back to the way we were. As far as the "preparation" for the collapse, part of our core beliefs is that Jesus will come back to earth after a period of great turmoil in the world. Some Christians think that the time is close and the dissolution of the U.S. is a sign.

Do you believe it was a sign?

I do not profess to know the will of God, but Revelation is explicit in saying that a lot of the nations will rise up and fight and that it will start in the Middle East. Just look at what happened to Israel in 2023 and what is still going on. It is not hard to see a clear line between current events and Scripture. I have told my congregation that there is nothing wrong with being prepared.

When you say the way, the U.S. used to be, I generally know what you are talking about but for our readers, can you elaborate?

I know it is not very "woke" to say what I am about to say, but when we started to focus on gender identity and transgender story hour, it rubbed a lot of my congregation the wrong way. And the fact that they were made to feel like they were homophobic or filled with hatred because we expect someone who is born a male to go by "he" and not have it be a guessing game. Also, we started putting the rights of non-citizens ahead of our own. I could go on and on. Fortunately, a lot of these issues are no longer issues with the various new political entities around the country. People have really gravitated towards their tribes. It has made things easier.

What do you say to the Americans or former Americans who are Muslims, Jews, or atheists who disagree with the theological view of the dissolution?

Look, our Founding Fathers enshrined religious freedoms in the Constitution. They are more than welcome to think and believe what they want to. There are a thousand theories and reasons why the U.S. collapsed. Mine just happens to be one that a lot of folks adhere to.

(TAHLEQUAH, OK) DEPUTY PRINCIPAL CHIEF OF THE CHEROKEE NATION, DAN CHEWEY

The Native American community was noticeably silent during the past several years as the U.S. became more polarized. I know you do not speak for every tribe, but you are the chief of one of the larger tribes in the U.S. Can you explain some of the more common views of the Native American community and how the dissolution has affected Native Americans?

Well, first, we have not been silent, everybody was just yelling louder! We knew that the breaking up of America would have a lot of unintended consequences for our people. It has taken us over a century to fight for the progress we have achieved in our communities. A lot of the hard-won programs were at the federal level and now we are having to renegotiate with individual states and confederations of states. In some places, we have lost ground, such as in South Carolina, where the Catawba tribe has lost some of its land and rights to their tribal courts which they had just started to gain before the U.S. dissolved. The smaller tribes have suffered the most setbacks, namely in the stripping of sovereignty laws. The Cherokee tribe is the largest, and we have more resources than others. We have been able to fight back against any encroachment on our land and sovereignty. I would say that the biggest setback has been the loss of collective strength that all the tribes brought to bear as a group when dealing with the federal government. Also, a lot of the aid programs, such as free college tuition and many of our tribal medical support that the federal government provided, have disappeared.

Were there any positive aspects to the Native American community when the U.S. ceased to exist? Did you personally support the dissolution?

Frankly, I do not see anything good coming out of this for our people. There was strength in numbers. I knew it would be not good for us. I am a veteran of the U.S. Army and the Afghanistan and Iraq wars. I have seen what happens to minorities when a country falls apart. They lose their minority rights and get blamed or face persecution. The safeguards are no longer there. If there is anything positive about it, it has made our tribe stronger as a people. It has forced us to be more self-reliant and develop our self-sufficient systems of support. For example, several of the largest tribes have banded together as a sort of our European Union to provide basic services such as health care and education for peoples of various tribes. The tribes that are better off financially can help the smaller tribes who do not have the resources. We help each other and are trying to fill the void of the federal government.

(LAS VEGAS, NV) SHANIA ATKINS, SOCIAL MEDIA INFLUENCER, ADULT ENTERTAINER, 7 THE "VOICE OF GENERATION Z"

Let me just start by asking what you have seen among the younger generations in the virtual world, which does not have boundaries. Are they upset with the breakup? Happy with it? Are they optimistic or pessimistic about their future?

Keep in mind that Generation Z and Millennials have both been repeatedly scarred by the September 11th attacks, the economic crisis of 2008, the chaotic four years of a Trump Presidency, and culminating with the breakup of the U.S. They are both very pessimistic generations who have repeatedly seen that "the American dream" of home ownership, a job that pays the bills and affords a few niceties, and each generation having it better than the last is a pipe dream.

They are more concerned with individual rights and jobs. They are talking with their feet, immigrating to places where there are more perceived freedoms as well as jobs; California and Florida.

The younger generations are not surprised by the breakup. They kind of saw it as inevitable. Nothing has turned out the way their parents told them it would in the U.S. They thought that they did the right things, i.e., going to college and going into the work force, but now they are saddled with debt and living at home with their parents.

You seem to be more left-leaning. What did you experience during the breakup, and why did you stay in Las Vegas?

Well, first, this is my home. I was born and raised here, and my family is here. I try to get along with everyone. I have learned to walk a fine line down the middle, but it has been challenging, especially in the virtual world.

When the breakup started, and Las Vegas wanted to go out on its own, I advocated against the breakup, and I received death threats. The scariest situation was when two men showed up at my house with weapons and started banging on my door. They were yelling at me to come outside and face the music. They called me a traitor and a woke terrorist. I called the police, and they left before the police arrived. I still received threats from them. For months after that, I had human feces smeared all over my front door. I installed visible cameras and got a big dog. That seemed to deter the visits. I always knew that when you put yourself out there on social media, you risked things like that, but it scared the hell out of me. I ended up buying a gun and learning how to use it from one of my followers. Something I thought I would never do.

Anything you want to say in closing?

Yes, we are stronger together than we are apart. I fear that this initial breakup is only the beginning. I see smaller interest groups now even more emboldened. I fear you will have cities and even neighborhoods breaking away so that in the next twenty years, you will have these lawless enclaves throughout what used to be the U.S.

(EAGLE PASS, TX) TROOPER MICHAEL MATTHEWS, FORMER OSCAR AWARD WINNING ACTOR & CURRENT TEXAS STATE TROOPER

Mr. Matthews, it is a pleasure to meet you. I have been a big fan of yours for years. I know you have always stayed close to your Texan roots. You grew up about an hour from here in Uvalde, TX and went to the University of Texas. You famously moved from Hollywood to Austin, TX, to raise your family. You won an Academy Award, and now you are a Texas State Trooper guarding the border. It seems like you have lived more than one life. May we live in interesting times. Can you tell us how the heck you ended up here?

I would not say that I "famously" moved to Austin. I didn't think Hollywood was the best place to raise kids in a normal way. I am a proud native Texan, and when duty calls, you answer. When the U.S. started collapsing, we started to have a surge in illegal immigrants. It was a free for all. The U.S. Border Patrol pretty much disintegrated. You had folks in the organization from all over the U.S. and they wanted to go back to their homes to protect their families. Also, there was a complete lack of guidance from Washington. I was down in Del Rio, which is along the border and could not believe the flood of immigrants. I had to stop my truck repeatedly to avoid hitting groups of migrants crossing the highway, and there was no one there to stop them. Governor Abbott sent in the National Guard, but they were quickly overwhelmed, too. There are just over 19,000 Texas National Guardsmen, and many of them had to take over the duties of several federal law enforcement and military organizations. Since Texas was on its own, it not only had to secure not only the border with Mexico, but the borders with Arkansas, Louisiana, New Mexico, and Oklahoma. Fortunately, we have formed our own separate country with Arkansas and Oklahoma, but at the time of the breakup, Texas needed to secure all of its borders.

Everybody needs a purpose and to step up when your community needs you. I did not see my acting abilities helping Texas much, and I have always had an interest in law enforcement, so here I am. During college, I planned to go to law school but realized that was not something that I wanted to do, and by sheer luck, I broke into acting. As a kid, I wanted to be a Texas Ranger, but you must have eight years under your belt as a State Trooper first, so I am starting at the ground floor. With a proud organization like the Rangers, you must earn your spurs first. I appreciate that. I know it is a long road, but it is something I want to do.

Please tell me about your official duties.

When the U.S. Border Patrol ceased to exist, and the Texas National Guard did not have the manpower to secure the borders, the Governor decided to have State Troopers take their place. I have been a Trooper now for over a year. I applied to Trooper Trainee Academy, spent 30 weeks there, and then was assigned to border duty at Eagle Pass. I just got out of my 12-month probationary period. My duties consist of roving patrols in the Eagle Pass area along the border. I will also man checkpoints along the main roads. We will detain illegals and check to see if they have any warrants. Under our current agreement with the Mexican government and governments of other countries down South, we will return them to their country of origin. Texas just does not have the resources to take care of all of them. If we stop them as they are crossing, we will stop them, get their biometric information, and turn them around.

Can you tell me about the Eagle Pass incident?

Well, first I was not there, I had just started the Academy, but we studied the heck out of it as a cautionary tale. Many of our instructors who taught us later in the course were there. During the turmoil at the border when the Border Patrol was disintegrating, the word got out that the border was open and not guarded, so illegal immigrants started flooding in. I think the most we had crossed in one day, and this is an estimate, was 8000 into Texas alone. At Eagle Pass, the remaining Border Patrol was overwhelmed. A company from the Texas National Guard showed up, and then a group of local bubbas armed to the teeth arrived. There were also Texas State Troopers present. Ultimately, there was a four-way standoff between the groups over who had the authority to be there. Tempers got the better of some folks, and someone started shooting. We still do not know who fired the first shot, but a several-hour firefight ensued. At the end of it, 20 people were killed, and dozens of others wounded. A group of detained illegals got caught in the crossfire, and two children were killed. The tally of those killed was two State Troopers, four National Guardsmen, one Border Patrol officer, nine militia members, and four detained migrants. That was the end of the U.S. Border Patrol's presence and existence in Texas. The militia members were arrested but subsequently pardoned by the Governor. It was a tragedy that will go down in Texas history as a dark day. Texans are killing Texans. Completely unnecessary and avoidable.

You have not mentioned your thoughts on the breakup of the U.S.

Unfortunately, I think we reached a point of no return many years ago. The only way for the U.S. to function and exist is through compromise at every level, from the federal government down to local boards of education. Compromise is based on trust and bargaining in good faith. Faith that even though I might disagree with a fellow American, at the end of the day, we both want a safe, free, and fair place to live and thrive and raise our families. We lost our faith in each other. Once you lose your faith, it is damn hard to get back, and it felt like every year there was something else to drive us apart. I saw it first hand when I dipped my toe into politics back in the 2010s. Both right and left were yelling past each other and demonizing the other side. When I tried to talk to folks of differing views, the loudest voices, which were also the angriest voices too, used words like "must", "no compromise", "evil", and un-American, and would hint at "doing what it takes" to keep America, America. Or America the way they saw it. It really worried me. There was no room for an informed minority view. That is dangerous for a democracy. I wish the U.S. had stayed together. Our strength was our unity, but we lost it. But after that initial foray, I wanted nothing to do with it. Too much venom and vitriol. One positive outcome of the dissolution is people and mini-states have coalesced around shared values and outlook on life so I doubt a collapse will happen again. I say all this knowing full well that several places through the former U.S. are in open conflict.

What do you think about the politics of Texas?

As an employee of the country of Texas, I support my government. Hell, I am directly protecting it! I think the government of Texarkana is upholding the values and traditions of the U.S. If anything, I think we are doing a better job of it since we see what the alternative is!

So, are politics in your future?

Ha, well, like I said, I had flirted with running for Governor back in the day, but now I am focused on being the best Trooper I can be.

That is not a hard no.

We will see.

(FREDERICKSBURG, VA) MAJOR DIMITRI TERPYLOV, UKRAINIAN REFUGEE, CURRENT SMALL BUSINESS OWNER & OFFICER IN THE VIRGINIA FREEDOM MILITIA

How did you come to America?

I came to the U.S. from Ukraine under the United for Ukraine visa program. I was part of the Azov Battalion in Mariupol, defending the city back in March 2022. I was severely wounded and one of the few casualties to be successfully evacuated before we had to surrender. I was evacuated by helicopter, and I thought we would be shot down at any moment. I really feel like God has been watching out for me at every turn. First, surviving Mariupol, then being evacuated, and finally making it to America.

How has your time been in the U.S.?

I love America, and that is why I am fighting for it. I am devastated by what has happened to the U.S. You have so many opportunities and freedoms here. Why would you throw that all away over silly political differences? You were the strongest country in the entire history of the world in every aspect. Why would you destroy that? America, with all its faults has always tried to do the right thing, and when it didn't, it tried to fix that flaw or would spend decades doing soul-searching. Some examples are slavery, civil rights, and the war in Vietnam, just to name a few.

I think I have a unique perspective on the dissolution of the U.S. I know what it is like to have to fight for the very existence of your country. I also know what it is like to not take my country for granted. I really think that Americans will regret breaking up. Nothing good will come of it in the long-run. If anything, you have just made the North American continent and much of the rest of the world more vulnerable, and it is open season for autocratic countries with strong militaries. Who will check their behavior? I have the answer: no one.

You are part of the Virginia Freedom Militia movement about?

Similar to what happened when Ukraine was first invaded by the Russians in 2014 in eastern Ukraine, several militia groups stepped up. We did the same in Virginia. When the U.S. started breaking up, there were a lot of grumblings and protests in the lower part of Virginia saying that they should go it alone and break away from the U.S. When violent protests started erupting in places like Richmond and Charlottesville, the Virginia National Guard had their hands full; especially protecting the National Capital Region. The Virginia Free Militia as stood up by several veterans to help assist in keeping the peace. At first, there was resistance from the Virginia governor, but when he realized that we were not a far-right movement, he had us vetted and made part of the Virginia State Guard. We have been patrolling the Virginia border and hinterland ever since. I could not just stand by without helping, especially with my significant military experience.

What is the status of the groups and individuals who want to break away from Virginia?

Fortunately, they are very disorganized and have several competing interests. Besides some isolated incidents like the firebombing of several DMVs and the heavy social media presence, they are not having much of an impact, in my opinion. But I will tell you from my experiences in Ukraine you cannot just ignore organizations like that. By the time they get big and powerful, it is too late to counter them.

Can you explain what has happened in Ukraine since the fall of the U.S.?

Yes, the U.S. cut back on aid to Ukraine drastically in 2024 and by the time the country dissolved, aid was non-existent. Things looked pretty bleak for Ukraine. Fortunately, three things happened. First, European countries and some of the strong democracies throughout the world stepped up to fill the void. Countries like Australia, India, Israel, Japan, and South Korea have been a lifeline to Ukraine. Secondly, Ukraine started to become more self-sufficient with its own domestic arms and tech industries. Fortunately, after our failed counteroffensive in 2023, we were able to build our defenses up and buy time to build our own domestic armaments capabilities and capacity. Ukraine was always an intellectual hub for the former Soviet Union and where most of our armaments were made. We had the know-how and the raw materials. It was just a matter of rebuilding the shuttered factories. Our tech industry, universities, and volunteers already had developed a cottage industry for drones and cyber warfare. Now, countries turn to us for the latest and greatest unmanned tech. Ukraine was an emerging tech hub before the war, so we have the in-house expertise. The hard part was just organizing it, harnessing it, and financing it.

What is the status of the war today?

Well, it is still a simmering conflict with relatively stable lines between Ukrainian forces and the Russian forces. We did manage to isolate Crimea with the repeated destruction of the bridge, and it has turned into a peninsula under siege. We do not expect it to return to Ukraine. I also think the rest of the land that the Russians occupy in Donbas is probably a loss, but Ukraine is in a relatively stable position militarily. Unfortunately, Russia has the size and resources to continue the fight indefinitely.

(WASHINGTON, DC, HEADQUARTERS OF THE NEW U.S. FEDERAL RESERVE) DR. PHIL WHITE, CURRENT CHAIR OF THE NEW U.S. FEDERAL RESERVE (AND FORMER CHAIR OF THE PREVIOUS U.S. FEDERAL RESERVE)

Dr. White, thank you for taking the time to talk with me. I know how busy you have been and currently are. You oversaw the breakup of the U.S. financial system and the collapse of a monetary system that had been the basic framework for the entire world's economy for over 80 years. The dissolution of the U.S. caused the world economy to go into a tailspin and we are currently in what many experts are calling the second Depression. Can you walk us through what happened when the U.S. financial system collapsed and its effects on the U.S. and world economies?

Thank you, this is an important story that needs to be explained to the public as a lesson learned and to prevent it from happening again. The saying used to be, "when the U.S. catches a cold, the whole world sneezes." In this case, the U.S. had leprosy, and the rest of the world caught it. It will take years, if not a decade, for the world economy to recover.

The thing that made this economic crisis different from any in the past, is the entire framework that the world monetary system is based on disintegrated. There was nothing to fall back on. Money is based on trust and confidence. A dollar bill is nothing more than a piece of paper that everyone accepts as currency. That acceptance was based on the faith that the U.S. government was stable. Think about it: money is a completely artificial construct with no intrinsic value. Its value is based on everyone buying into its value. When the U.S. started falling apart, that faith went away, and nothing immediately took its place. Overnight, people's savings worldwide were worth nothing. Most governments had bought billions of U.S. dollars of U.S. bonds over the decades after World War II. U.S. dollars backed their entire economies. Think about it: the value of everything went into freefall. Everything from stocks to gas to eggs. People's pay became useless. Our modern economic system is based on specialization. If you are a teacher or a car mechanic, you don't have to worry about growing food or making clothes because you can pay others to do that. You can focus on becoming an expert in your field.

The collapse started even before the U.S. dissolved. Everything was based on trust, and the markets were based on emotions. The stock markets worldwide started tanking and went into freefall. On Bloody Monday, every stock exchange in the world shut down within hours of opening. That has never happened in the history of the world. The U.S. dollar went from the world's most stable and trusted currency to as valuable as a Weimar Republik Deutschemark. The safeguards to keep countries' economies from going into a tailspin, such as a cash infusion by the World Bank, were based on the dollar. The EU Central Bank had its hands full just trying to take care of its member countries, much less the U.S. All currencies were in flux. Our credit rating went from AA+ to CCC+ in a matter of weeks. For the point of reference, Germany's credit rating is AAA, the highest. China's rating is A+, and countries like Pakistan or Ukraine are CCC+.

Overnight, the U.S. economy became a barter economy in many places. The dollar was no longer trusted or accepted. If you did not have a valuable skill or did not produce a necessity such as food, you were out of luck. Microeconomies started forming. Most economies throughout the politic entities that now comprise the former U.S. states have stabilized somewhat, but there are still scars.

Can you give us some examples of the more innovative ways that this happened?

California. California proved to be the most adept at quickly forming a new economic system. They immediately started buying up Canadian Dollars and that became their currency of choice. Of course, there was a shortage of paper currency, but the Governor of California cut a deal with the Canadian Prime Minister where a lot of the food stuffs they produced were sent to Canada instead of the normal customers throughout the U.S. California grows most of the U.S.'s produce. As a result, we had food shortages throughout the rest of the U.S., and prices for basic fruits and vegetables skyrocketed.

Are any outliers that have success using novel approaches?

Florida starting the Florida dollar backed by the Euro. It has actually been one of the more stable currencies.

What were some of the unexpected crises?

The biggest one was over water rights in the southwest. Without the federal government to referee, the disputes between Arizona, California, Colorado, New Mexico, Nevada, Utah, and Wyoming turned violent. Also, you have all the Native American tribes that claim they have never used or received the allocation from the Colorado River that they are due.

Right now, most of the mini-states that comprise what used to be the U.S. are suffering from hyperinflation. Prices for everything are sky-high, and our entire supply chain has been disrupted, from the banking system to the transportation of goods. Also, federal organizations such as the FTC, the SEC, and the Fed are no longer overseeing the entire U.S. They are still present in the rump U.S. country, but not in other places.

What industries and businesses have weathered the collapse or even thrived?

Many of the big box stories are doing okay. Their costs are significantly up and their selections have been drastically reduced, but people are visiting those stores more than before the collapse. Many online retailers ceased to exist due to the disruption of the shipping industry. Regular brick-and-mortar stores regained primacy.

If we talk about industries that have survived or even thrived, the "sin industries" have done the best so far. Gun and ammo sales have gone through the roof, as well as alcohol and marijuana sales as well as online pornography. Smoking has had a resurgence in the former U.S., so tobacco companies are doing well, unfortunately. Any industry that is tied to self-sufficiency, such as solar and wind energy systems, has seen a huge surge in demand. People are worried that governments will no longer provide for their basic needs as far as electricity or security.

What is the way ahead?

The way ahead is trade deals and what I am pushing for. An EU-like construct to cut down the trade barriers and tariffs; have a shared currency and banking system, and regulations that safeguard investors and consumers. It is an uphill battle. Emotions are still raw between the mini-states and there is a lot of hostility between, for example, the California state (UWCF) and Greater Idaho/New Washington. They just see each other as enemies, and the Idaho folks are assisting insurgents in open rebellion against the government in Sacramento. It will take time. Keep in mind that after World War II, it took until the 1990s to develop the EU and share a common currency fully. And even then, several countries opted out like the UK. We are in preliminary talks with several other mini-states about forming a trade union.

(OUTSIDE OF GREAT FALLS, MT) HEADMAN STAN GENEGA, LEADER OF THE EDEN COMMUNITY, AN SELF-SUFFICIENT AUTONOMOUS VILLAGE

Stan's compound covers several square miles of rugged, mountainous area and, according to him, completely self-sufficient. Stan, your compound is quite impressive. I am a former soldier and outdoorsman, and I have not seen anything like this before. Can you tell me about your compound?

We are proud of what we have built here. This is the culmination of 15 years of work. When we first started here, it just consisted of a few trailers, RVs, and some generators in an area we cleared about the size of a football field. We were definitely not self-sufficient then and learned to do without. Now, the only things that we have to "get from town" are modern electronics, microchips, some medicines such as antibiotics, some fuel and vehicles, parts, and clothes. Everything else is produced here. Do not get the wrong impression. We are not a 19th-century community. We have all the modern technology. We just choose to be able to maintain it on our as much as we can. We produce our electricity through solar and windmill farms on the mountainside. We also produce some electricity through hydroelectric power running from the river.

We produce our food year-round with our extensive greenhouses and self-sustaining bison herd, goats, sheep, and, of course, chickens. Our dairy products come from our goats, and we produce wool from the sheep for clothing if we want.

Much of medicine is produced in the greenhouses and comes from nature. We have our clinic with a doctor, paramedics, herbologist, and midwife. Like I said, what we cannot produce, we stockpile from Great Falls.

We have a fleet of trucks, cars, ATVs, motorcycles, and even light aircraft. We have a machine shop and 3D printers to help with parts. Most of our vehicles are put together using motor vehicle technology from before computers so we can fix them ourselves. We use propane or batteries to power most of them.

We have a school, K-12, that we are very proud of. I would stack our curriculum and students against any charter school in Great Falls. As a matter of fact, we have had members of the school board visit us to see why are students are so successful. Our curriculum is based on the classical education model of focusing on logic and rhetoric, and students are required to develop their curriculums. A lot of what they learn is self-taught with expertise from our community and focuses on maintaining our self-sufficiency with a deep understanding of how technology works and can repaired or improved upon. We really focus on our students understanding the engineering and science behind things. We have a mathematician, physicist, several engineers, a former English professor, a computer scientist, Green Berets, farmers, and a doctor. There is a core curriculum they must follow to ensure they have the basic skills of reading, writing, and a dose of STEM. All our students are required to have a firm foundation in STEM. It is how our community survives and thrives, having the expertise to expand. We also require practical skills, including medical and farming. We are teaching our students to be self-sustaining. They can branch out in almost any area they want. It could be electric engineering or computer science, gunsmithing, medicine, etc. We have a mentorship program once a student reaches the 7th grade, where a member of the community takes him under his wing and treats him almost like an apprentice. Our kids are free to leave the community when they turn 18, but most choose to stay or go out into the world and return.

Every member of our community has a specific job and then general duties. Also, for every primary person, we have at least one backup. We used to have that set up on Special Forces' teams where you would have a senior and junior medic.

All of this sounds great, but how do you answer critics who say you are running a right-wing cult that is preparing for the end of the world?

Look, we are a group of like-minded people who are concerned about the future of society and foresee trouble ahead. Just look at this election and the aftermath. We have open conflict in the U.S. This has not happened since the Civil War. We are just prepared, that is all. Our people are free to leave anytime they want. We have folks from all walks of life and beliefs. We have Christians, atheists, Muslims, Buddhists, you name it. We have gay, straight, liberal, conservative, and we do not discriminate. As long as you adhere to our rules and actively contribute to our society, we are fine with it. We pay our taxes and just want to be left alone.

What about the standoff several years ago with the ATF, FBI, and U.S. Marshals over charges that you had modified illegal weapons?

First, that ended peacefully, and all of the weapons we have and had been legal. We just had a disgruntled former member who was kicked out for harassing other members. He held a grudge and made several accusations against us. We do have fully automatic weapons, but they are completely legal. We have members, including myself, who have a Federal Firearms License to own and sell automatic weapons. We have not modified anything illegally. Even when folding stocks were deemed illegal back in 2023, we applied for the ATF tax stamps, so we are fully legal.

What are your political views, and what do you think of the dissolution of the U.S.?

The best way to describe us is ultra-libertarian. We do not like government interfering with our personal lives. We do not vote or participate in government beyond paying our taxes and following the laws of the state of Montana and local governments. We have our council of elders and our economic system based on bartering. I do not understand why our way of life is a threat to those on the outside. As you can see by your visit, we are totally transparent and have let you see anything you want and talk to whoever you want.

As far as the dissolution of the U.S., it really does not affect us. Governments come and go. It is the tribes and families that last. We are a tribe and a family, and we will not just survive. As you can see, we are thriving. If anything, the events of the past two years have proved us right. We have to turn away potential members constantly, and there is a waiting list to join our community!

(FALLS CHURCH, VA, JUST OUTSIDE OF WASHINGTON, DC) U.S. NAVY CAPTAIN JOHN SIMPSON, FORMER NASA ASTRONAUT

Captain Simpson, thank you for taking the time to speak with me. Your story is unique, and some would say epic. You were onboarding the International Space Station (ISS) when the U.S. started breaking up and had to deal with not only internal U.S. (or former U.S.) politics but also international politics with the Russians. Can you explain what happened on ISS?

I was the ISS Commander when the post-election turmoil started. We had a grew of six, two Americans, two Russians, a German, and a Japanese. You become a brotherhood up there, and geopolitics is put aside for the sake of the mission and comradeship. Paul Schmitt, the other American, and I were watching with alarm at what was happening. As you know, the main nodes of NASA are spread across the U.S. We launched from Cape Canaveral, Florida and mission control is in Houston, Texas. NASA is a U.S. government agency. So, post-breakup, you are dealing with three separate governments where there used to be one. Throw in the Russians and you now are dealing with four. The space community is tight-knit, and we try to keep politics away from focusing on the mission, but it was unavoidable then. We ended up being caught in the middle. The governments of Florida, Texas, and what remained of the U.S. were fighting over ownership of the space program. NASA cannot function without money either, so you had a case where Texas said Houston is under their control and Florida said Cape Canaveral is theirs, so the U.S. said, okay, fine, then you knew entities pay for it. We were stuck in limbo. Then you had the Russian government try and do a powerplay and take over ISS. We had long discussions with the Russian government about how we continued cooperation when the Soviet Union collapsed, and we did not try and take advantage of the situation then.

Where were your loyalties at the time?

I am a U.S. military officer who took an oath to support and defend the Constitution of the U.S., so my allegiances were and are with the U.S. My family lived in Florida at the time, and to add to the tug-of-war, I am a Texas A&M graduate and native Texan. In my mind, there was no question of who I worked for, but family and friends thought otherwise. I had the governor of Florida reach out to me, stating that if I stayed with Florida, he would make me a senior leader in Florida's space agency, Florida Space Agency (FSA).

How did it all end?

All the governments involved decided that for the sake of humanity and science, to put aside differences and cooperate. We were stuck on ISS for six months longer than planned. Fortunately, we had the reliable Russian Soyuz capsules available, and that is how we got home.

What is the current state of the space program across the former U.S.?

It is in disarray. For the first time, there are no Americans, or what used to be Americans, onboard the ISS. And now you have multiple space agencies with not enough resources to be on their own. You have the remainder of the U.S. that "owns" NASA with a facility in Maryland but no ability to launch anything, then Florida with the FSA that has the launch vehicles but not the financial resources or all the technical aspects that the other major NASA locations brought to bear, and finally Texas with Houston, who has the technical expertise, but without the resources. Also add in the facilities in Huntsville, Alabama, and you can see that the once robust U.S. space program is defunct. It is disheartening that just when we were getting over the 50-year lull in advances in space, NASA died. I do think private industry will really take the lead more than it has. The best chances of success are from SpaceX, and fortunately for Texas, they have launch facilities there. This might be the end of government importance in the space program. The Russians just do not have the resources to go out completely on their own, and the Chinese have the resources but not necessarily the expertise and until recently, they do not play well with others. Finally, you have the European Space Agency (ESA), which has the best chance for governmental success along with the Chinese. It is interesting to see the new ESA/Chinese collaboration efforts coupled with private industry in Europe and China as they all try and overcome prejudices and suspicions and develop trust.

(CLEVELAND, OHIO POLICE HQ) CLEVELAND CHIEF OF POLICE LOUIS GREENBERG

Chief Greenberg, you have been the Cleveland Police Chief for the past five years and are well respected in the community. Can you tell us what is happening in your city?

It really is tragic once both houses of the Ohio General Assembly voted to secede, Cleveland exploded into violent protests in opposition to the legislation. Similar to the situation in Atlanta, many citizens in Cleveland felt disenfranchised, and they were worried that since most of the citizens were black, things would get bad for them. We have violence, but nothing like Atlanta or Chicago. It could have been a lot worse. Fortunately, our prominent citizens, especially professional sports figures and church leaders, really stepped up. We even had street gang leaders making appeals to stop the violence. The "This is our home" campaign really took off after programs for teens made a difference. If you had a choice between torching a police car or spending an afternoon playing basketball with a member of the Cleveland Cavaliers, what would you choose?

We also partnered with local community colleges and trade schools to offer free courses that would provide citizens with a skill. Each school is sponsored by either a sports team, a church or a business. These sponsors help provide a stipend and housing while students are in school. Of course, part of the program is they must work in a job that benefits the community or is tied to their field of study. When people are secure with their lives and are able to provide for themselves and their families, they are less likely to jeopardize that with street violence.

What recommendations would you have for the mayors of Atlanta and Chicago who are experiencing unprecedented violence?

Their situations are a lot different. Atlanta is dealing with a full-scale insurgency, and Chicago is fighting against the state of Illinois. I would say to the state governments in Georgia and Illinois the solution will not be based on strong police or military action alone. Also, the more killings that happen only make it more difficult to find a peaceful resolution ultimately.

(NORFOLK, VA, NAVAL STATION NORFOLK) U.S. ADMIRAL JOHN RITTENBERG DISCUSSES THE USS ALABAMA INCIDENT

The story behind the rogue nuclear-powered and armed submarine USS Alabama has not yet been fully told. Much of it is still classified. We are sitting with U.S. Admiral John Rittenberg, who led the combined U.S./NATO naval task force that tracked down the USS Alabama and sunk it. Admiral, can you tell us what happened and the current situation with what was the U.S. Navy?

Sure, I can tell you what I can to the best of my ability. Keep in mind that there were a lot of moving parts and thousands of airmen, sailors, soldiers, and marines involved from ten countries, as well as over 50 ships. If you interview anyone directly involved, they will give you a different story that is not wrong. It is just from their perspective and the information they received as events transpired.

When the U.S. started dissolving, the Department of Defense and Energy took it upon themselves to consolidate all our nuclear weapons. We had them spread out in missile silos out west, in bunkers in Europe, in storage facilities on Air Force bases in the continental U.S., and of course, in submarines silently patrolling underneath the oceans of the world. We thought the toughest part would be getting back our overseas assets, we did not even conceive that some submarine commander along with his crew would go rogue. I do think there was some serious mental instability ongoing, but we will never know for sure.

What we do know is that all of our boomers, our nickname for submarines carrying nuclear weapons, responded when we gave the recall order. All except for the USS Alabama that was patrolling the northern Atlantic Ocean. It is not unusual for subs to miss communications windows for a variety of reasons. We started getting concerned after a couple of days with no contact. We assumed the worst and thought the sub had suffered some catastrophe. We started search efforts after 24 hours of no communication. Forty-eight hours after we initially tried to contact Alabama with recall orders, we got a message from them. It said, and I am paraphrasing, that they did not recognize the U.S. military chain of command as legitimate and were waiting for the proper authorities to contact them. In the meantime, they would continue to run silent, and any attempt to force them to the surface would be seen as an act of war.

Our boomer commanders are carefully selected and given a lot of leeway in how they operate for obvious reasons. They literally could start World War III on their own. Of course, we have launch code safeguards, but there are ways to bypass them, especially for someone who has over 20 years of experience operating submarines. In order for them to launch, he would need to co-opt his second in command.

In the entire history of the U.S.'s silent service, we have never had a mutiny or captain go rogue. Of course, we prepare contingencies for such a situation, but still, you have to find them.

And that is exactly what we did. With our allies in NATO, we assembled several task forces throughout the Atlantic to look for them. NATO has robust anti-submarine capabilities, and we train all the time to look for subs.

We knew that the Alabama would eventually run out of food and have to surface. They could just stay still and silent and the chances of finding them were slim, but as soon as they made a break for a place to resupply, they might create some signature we could pick up on. Their options for places to resupply were limited, and our best guess was that they would try a surreptitious resupply with a country that would not ask questions. Our task force honed in on nations without the best relationships with the U.S. in and around the Atlantic, such as Cuba and Venezuela. And that is exactly what happened. After four months, they surfaced near Cuba, and our sensors picked up on them. We quickly moved a task force into the area and attempted to communicate with them. The communications with them were very hostile, and the captain said if we got any closer or did anything aggressive, they would launch all of their missiles. The President of the U.S. decided at the time that we could not chance that happening, so using precision strikes from surface ships and planes, sunk the USS Alabama as it attempted to dive.

Did you ever recover the nuclear weapons or what was left of them?

I am not at liberty to discuss that. I will say that the threat to the world was eliminated. It was gut-wrenching to have to kill our fellow sailors and countrymen. 156 U.S. sailors were onboarding the USS Alabama, and I can imagine some of them were unwilling participants in this mutiny. The decision to sink the Alabama will haunt me for the rest of my life.

(PHILADELPHIA, PA) OWNER OF A CHAIN OF GROCERY STORES ALONG THE EAST COAST, "JIM," LAST NAME WITHHELD FOR PRIVACY CONCERNS AND TO AVOID DISAGREEMENTS WITH DISTRIBUTORS

One negative repercussion of the breakup of the U.S. that has not gotten the attention it deserves but has affected every American (or former American) is the disruption in the supply chain. It has caused massive food shortages and shortages of everything. Can you tell us what the repercussions are to your business and what is the situation now?

Yes, absolutely. Americans had gotten used to living in the land of plenty and being able to purchase anything anytime they wanted and having it delivered, in some cases within 24 hours. Think about the network of delivery drivers across the country who worked for Amazon, FedEx, UPS, or even the U.S. post office. This system was based on free trade, open borders, a common currency, and a shared banking system. Now, that system has been completely upended.

When the U.S. started to collapse, many states closed their borders and, in some cases, added tariffs or treated going across a state boundary as if you were crossing an international border. Think about something simple like fruits and vegetables. Most of the vegetables that we enjoy year-round, like spinach, are grown near Salinas, California. Just think of how we would take for granted that we would always have fresh spinach available to us. It takes about a week or two from the time you harvest spinach for it to start to wilt and go bad. Our system of commerce and delivery was so efficient you could have spinach on the shelves of grocery stores in North Carolina within 72 hours of it being picked; all the way from California. It was delivered by truck, and those trucks relied on a highway system that did not stop you every time you crossed a state line.

Now, fruits and vegetables are spoiling before they can get to the consumer due to all of these new borders and restrictions on the free movement of goods and services. Also, the prices for everything have tripled and quadrupled in some cases. Amazon filed for bankruptcy six months ago. Their margins were very tight already, and they relied on sheer volume to make a profit. Now, with the myriad of new regulations, currencies, and banking regulations, it was impossible to provide the same service in all 50 of the former states. Not only did they have to pay state taxes, but they also had to pay tariffs, and each new mini-state instituted complicated laws on most goods and services. Amazon just could not keep up. So now the land of the plenty is the land of shortages. At any given time at any one of my stores, half the shelves are empty. It is one thing not to have 20 different choices for soda, but it is another thing when you do not have baby formula or diapers or the prescription drugs that keep you alive. It is a tragedy, and I do not think the states that were crying for secession thought this through and how good we really had it. Were our divisions so bad to justify the breaking up of the most powerful country in the history of the world?

How are you overcoming these shortages and working through all the morass of different mini-state laws and regulations to get your shelves stocked?

We have to drastically cut down on the number of choices that were used for stocking. Now, instead of ten different types of Ranch dressing, you might be lucky to have two types of salad dressing on your shelves. That is just the way it is. I have heard that it is reminiscent of grocery shopping in the former Soviet Union. We will have runs on the stores when a scarce item comes in. There are several apps now that will alert you when a popular item is about to hit the shelves. Oreo cookies, of all things, are one of those items, along with steaks.

I have to negotiate trade deals with distributors in other states personally and some cases, lobby their state legislators to allow our stores to get special dispensation for the delivery of goods. Another unintended consequence is the rise in corruption. It took most of the history of the U.S. to change the culture where corruption is frowned upon. Now, it is just the price of doing business. Everyone has their hand out. That is one of a myriad of reasons the prices of everything have gone up.

Has there been any other unintended consequences for conducting business from the dissolution of the U.S. that you have seen?

Yes, several. The banking system is in disarray. The U.S. had the Federal Reserve, FDIC, and the SEC to protect consumers and monitor the health of our economy. Now, there are no overarching oversight mechanisms for this assortment of political entities that now compromise the former boundaries of the U.S. Trying to make payments from one to the other is now like conducting international transactions, so subject to different laws and systems. We are already experiencing widespread inflation and the beginnings of a recession. I am concerned that it is just a matter of time before we have hyperinflation and possibly a depression. We had no idea the Pandora's box we opened by breaking up the U.S. But what did people expect??

(MINNEAPOLIS, MN) ERIK WILDER, HOST OF THE PODCAST "MINNESOTA, EH", SOCIAL MEDIA INFLUENCER & ADVOCATE FOR MERGING WITH CANADA

Eric, you have led the grassroots effort in Minnesota to form some sort of relationship with Canada. You are the only former state even to consider something like that. Can you tell us why and why so many Minnesotans support it?

Minnesotans have always been a pragmatic bunch. It was first settled by immigrants from the Nordic countries so a hearty bunch. Politically, we have been reliably Democrat which is not the norm for this part of the country. Our politics tend to align with our neighbors to the north as opposed to those to the west, east, and south of us. We even have the accent!

When the musical chairs started when the U.S. started to disintegrate, we Minnesotans looked around and did not really see a place for us to land. The closest states that are aligned with us politically are on the coasts. It is kind of hard to be part of a country and not share a border. We share the Canadian pragmatism and liberal outlook on mankind.

We are fortunate we live in a land full of natural resources with amazing natural beauty. As such, we are very conscious of how we treat the environment, and Canada's policies are closer to ours.

So, in typical Minnesotan fashion, we had a good public debate. I was not the first person to come up with the idea, but I was one of the first to be taken seriously about it.

I am like the Joe Rogan and John Stewart of Minnesota and my popularity is based on a mix of issues of the day important to Minnesotans coupled with entertainment. I brought on a gentleman who gave a compelling argument to somehow partner with Canada. It really got my attention, and I am a major advocate for it. Canada talk started when it appeared that there was no way out of this election mess. And by the time states started seceding in mass, we, Minnesotans had already been debating it for months. Remember the tongue and cheek TikTok series that went viral? It compared and contrasted Canadians and Minnesotans and was hilarious. I think that did not do more to gain support for the initiative than anything else.

We have a convoluted way of getting statewide ballot initiatives on the ballot. They are actually called amendments. It went through the state legislature first then on to a ballot measure. It basically gave voters three choices, and for any to pass, it had to have a supermajority of 60%. That is a high bar. The choices were: 1) go it alone, 2) start the process to become a new province of Canada, or 3) enter negotiations for an EU-type supranational organization. On August 24, 2024, by 68%, Minnesotans picked the EU-like option with a voter turnout of 81%! Impressive. So that is where we are. It will become official in 2027, but most of the rules and agreements are already in place.

What are the biggest differences between the U.S. and Canadian governments?

The metric system! That is #1 with a bullet. We are actually getting a lot of resistance from trying to go metric, but if that is the least of our problems, I will take it.

True free healthcare is the other major difference.

(BOISE, ID, IDAHO STATE LEGISLATURE) STATE SENATOR DON SAMPSON, LEADER OF THE IDAHO SECESSIONIST MOVEMENT

Senator Sampson, you led the efforts in the Idaho Assembly for secession that ultimately led to Idaho being the first state to secede. A cascade of other states followed that. What prompted you to push for secession? Didn't the American Civil War put that issue to bed for good?

A lot of pundits misunderstood the reasons behind the secession movement and the legal framework that supported it. It is a very emotional question, and those emotions are tied to our history. Yes, the Civil War did finally solve the question of secession, but for completely different reasons than now. The States of the Confederacy seceded over the issue of slavery, plain and simple. You can couch it as States' rights, but it was tied to a state's right to continue the institution of slavery. It was an act of rebellion and in support of a cause, slavery, that was morally corrupt. It went against our basic principles that "all men are created equal."

Secession 2025 is based on the failure of the government to perform its basic duties as well as an unconstitutional election. I am a lawyer and a member of the Idaho Legislature so I follow the rule of law in the performance of my duties. The Constitution is a contract between the U.S. government and the U.S. states and citizens. It basically says the federal government has the following duties, responsibilities, and authorities, and those not specifically stated are the states. The first paragraph implies the U.S.'s power is given to them by its citizens. "We, the people of the United States, in Order to form a more perfect Union, establish Justice, ensure domestic Tranquility, provide for the common defense…". Those three responsibilities of the government bequeathed to them by the citizens are the top three things the government must do. What happens when the government fails to do them repeatedly? Justice, look at the 2024 Presidential mess. No one can argue that the results are not in dispute.

You have four courts, with two saying the election did not violate the Constitution and two saying it did. Furthermore, you had the U.S. Supreme Court, God rest their souls, refusing to make a ruling on it. When the Supreme Court decides not to rule on a case, it means that the lower court rulings stand. And in this case, the results were split. Domestic Tranquility: can anyone with a straight face say that the U.S. is experiencing peaceful coexistence? In January and February 2024, you had violence breaking out in almost every major city in the U.S., and places like Atlanta, northern California, Chicago, and western North Carolina are still on fire. Finally, providing for the common defense was tied to not only the widespread and uncontrolled violence across the country, which the federal government failed to stop but also the crisis at the border for the past several years.

But didn't President Harris invoke the Insurrection Act and try and activate the National Guard nationwide to restore order?

I prefer you do not call her "president" for obvious reasons. She did not have the authority to invoke the Insurrection Act since she was legally not president. The U.S. was too far gone. The federal government was not able to perform its Constitutionally enshrined duties. This was not the case during the Civil War. The government was still functioning. I argue, should we have kept sputtering along with half the country not recognizing the legitimacy of Harris? It was dysfunctional, and if a house is rotten to the core, you have to tear it down to rebuild again. That is exactly what we did. Is it perfect? No. Do I wish that we did not have to go the secession route? Yes. It breaks my heart. Now, you have multiple confederations, countries, and independent states where the values of the citizenry are more closely aligned. I argue that given time, most of the former U.S. will become more stable in contrast to the last few years of the U.S.

Do you have any regrets about starting the movement that led to the dissolution of the U.S.?

Of course, I do. I am a veteran of the U.S. Navy, my son served in the Army, my father was killed Vietnam, and my grandfather was a wounded Korean War veteran. My family literally spilled blood in support of the U.S. We were patriots. But life sometimes comes down to hard choices, and when a relationship is not helping but hurting, you have to end it. It is always messy and emotional, but I am sure that I did the right thing. It will be up to my Maker to decide my final judgment.

(DENVER, CO) JANE AUSTIN, MARIJUANA DISPENSARY OWNER & CIVIL RIGHTS ADVOCATE DISCUSSES THE CURRENT STATUS OF SOCIAL JUSTICE MOVEMENTS IN THE FORMER U.S.

Ms. Sampson, you were heavily involved with some of the major social justice movements prior to the collapse of the U.S. Can you tell us the state of those movements and civil rights overall? I know you have maintained your formerly nationwide network of activists.

It really depends upon where you live. With the fracturing of the U.S., social justice movements fragmented as well. In social justice movements, there is strength in numbers unfortunately, so we had some major setbacks. As a black and brown person, I was part of the Black Lives Matter movement. Once all the turmoil started in the U.S., civil rights for any group went on the back burner. I get it. We were focused on our survival as a nation. But as soon as the musical chairs stopped, we saw the resurgence of some disturbing trends, like the movement to use the old Confederate battle flag as the flag of the U.S.S. Not good. There was a lot of thinly veiled racial undertones about the whole campaign. In the cities under siege, Atlanta, Chicago, and Cleveland, you have a predominantly black population not agreeing with the state officials' decision to breakaway. And in two out of three cases, heavy-handed practices just increased the anger amongst the populace and the violence.

We are seeing a disturbing trend with the "revamping" of school -curriculum in places like South Carolina to lessen the discussion of slavery.

It seems like you are really honing in on the U.S.S.

It has been most egregious there. Random checkpoints routinely stop black and brown people much more than whites. We used to teach our sons about "driving while black." Now we have to teach them it all over again and also fill in the education gaps where schools are cutting curriculum about our heritage.

What do you say to the people who blame black citizens for the violence? They point out that black people are destroying their own neighborhoods.

First, I always preach non-violence as option number 1. I also agree that you shouldn't destroy your neighborhoods. BUT you should appreciate the frustration of a black man or woman living in downtown Atlanta. Constantly concerned with getting taken in for questioning just because you are walking down the street.

Where are some places that are getting it right and social justice is thriving?

There are the usual suspects such as the UWCF out in California as well as the new U.S. A big surprise is Utah. Once they became their political entity, they really embraced diverse views and health for society. They passed a gay marriage amendment to their Constitution! Would you have even remotely considered that happening in Utah five years ago?

Speaking of gay rights, again, the U.S.S. is leading the way with discrimination laws. Wanting to put gay sex laws back on the books. Texarkana is another one that has taken a step back with gay rights. But then you see places like Florida and Utah which have surprised us with their openness and tolerance. Utah has even included gay rights in its own Bill of Rights.

Could you sum up the social justice and civil rights movements across the former U.S. post-breakup?

We have seen a retreat of peoples into their "tribes." Each of the new legal entities has become more entrenched in their views. Also there has been the mass migrations of people to enclaves that more closely mirror their beliefs. The more progressive places like U.W.C.F and the new U.S. are beacons of progressive causes, whereas more conservative areas like Texarkana or the U.S.S. have set back civil rights and other key social issues such as women's reproductive rights to a different era. You really cannot get an abortion in those two places. Some pundits will say things are better and more stable now, but I think long-term not. Our diversity was our strength despite the anger.

How is the marijuana business?

Thriving! Colorado was the first state to legalize recreational marijuana, so it paved the way for others to follow. We made all the first mistakes and have the most mature business model. I do not think the industry was adversely affected at all. People still want their escapes, and if anything, we experienced growth. My mom-and-pop place has seen an 8% increase in sales since 2024.

(BATAVIA, NY, UPSTATE NY) NAME WITHHELD, LOCAL MILITIA MEMBER & SCHOOL TEACHER

We are meeting with "Jill" at an undisclosed location in Upstate New York. She is a member of a local underground militia group that is against the governments in Albany, NY and Washington, DC. And also, a school teacher. Jill, could you state the goals of your group and your activities?

We are against the illegal governments in Albany and DC. These governments do not represent the people and values of the population of Upstate New York. When the U.S. no longer existed, we should have had a referendum on our future. The Upstate of New York has always been very different from New York City and the other major towns. We are more traditional and conservative. Unfortunately, our voices have always been dismissed. We really thought this would be our chance to go our way, just like it has happened all across the former U.S.

Our goal is simple: we want a binding referendum put to a vote about breaking away several counties in Upstate New York into our own country. Let the people decide.

Our activities started peacefully, with social media posts and protests in Albany, but they have fallen on deaf ears. We are small but committed. We have committed small acts of violence but have not hurt anyone. Unfortunately, violence is the only way for us to be heard.

Your group has claimed responsibility for bombings at several DMVs and National Guard armories across northern New York state. Is that correct?

Yes, we have always provided a warning first, with just enough time to evacuate anybody present. Our goal, as stated, is to be heard.

You mentioned that the people in the Upstate of New York are more conservative and traditional than in other parts of New York. Can you provide more details?

Yes, we are against the woke agenda and the liberal causes that have been forced down our throats by Albany. Batavia and New York City might as well be on different planets. Forcing us to have "gender-neutral" bathrooms is beyond ridiculous. We believe that God made two genders, not three, five, or ten. As a teacher, I became very alarmed when the 2021 New York Department of

Education policy on "educational equity" pushed critical race theory on us. We want to have a say in how our children are taught. Our communities are not well off. We cannot just send our kids to private schools or homeschool them. We are working-class people who live paycheck to paycheck, so both parents must work. When I was growing up, the curriculum in schools reflected the values, norms, traditions, and culture of our local community. Yes, certain subjects were dictated by the state, but they were value-neutral and were important skills to know, such as mathematics and the ability to read and write. As a teacher, I have very little leeway in what I can teach, and that is not right. It is hard to teach subjects or biased topics that you do not believe in. I have no problem teaching different sides of an issue. I think it is an important part of education, but when it is one-sided, that is wrong, especially with a subject like critical race theory that insinuates to our mostly white students that their ancestor's treatment of minorities is to blame for any perceived injustices today. We just want to be left alone to run our affairs.

(WASHINGTON, DC, HEADQUARTERS OF THE DEPARTMENT OF HEALTH & HUMAN SERVICES) DR. WARREN KOCH, CURRENT SECRETARY OF THE DEPARTMENT OF HEALTH & HUMAN SERVICES (HHS) FOR THE NEW U.S. & FORMER U.S. SURGEON GENERAL, ON THE REPERCUSSIONS TO U.S. HEALTHCARE AS A RESULT OF THE DISSOLUTION OF THE U.S.

Dr. Koch, you have a very lengthy medical career in the public sector. Among your many accolades includes being one of the first researchers on the ground in Africa for the World Health Organization during the AIDS crisis in the early nineties. Back when AIDS was a death sentence, and the stigma was so negative, many of your colleagues stayed away from the subject. You were on the Presential COVID Advisory Board and for the last two years of the existence of the U.S., you were the last U.S. Surgeon General. You are currently serving as the Secretary for HHS in the new U.S. or what is left of it. Can you discuss the repercussions of the breakup for the U.S. healthcare system as well as the current state of general physical and mental for what is now the former U.S.?

Well, that is a tall order. I will do my best to explain the current situation across the former states. Our healthcare system is in complete disarray and has collapsed in some of the lower-income parts of the country, especially in rural areas. We have recovered somewhat, but it is now a patchwork system of haves and have-nots. Our healthcare system has always favored the well-off, but the disparity is even worse now. Under the old system, we had nationwide HMOs as well as regional HMOs. Oversight of our healthcare system was the responsibility of the HHS, and its various agencies and offices are the implementers. For example, the FDA oversaw the safety and efficacy of medications. That system is now gone. The CDC, who maintained constant vigilance over our health no longer overwatches all the states. We have these rump agencies left, but they are just a shadow of what they previously were in terms of capabilities and capacities. All of the federal departments experienced a massive brain drain when the U.S. collapsed. Healthcare in every corner of the former U.S. has been adversely affected. In some places, it is nonexistent. Some of the hardest hit areas are those that relied on the federal government for healthcare, like Indian reservations. That system has collapsed. Rural clinics in every former state were subsidized by the federal government. Fortunately, many of the Native American tribes are banding together to form their own HMO. It might be a test model for others to emulate.

As a result of the collapse of the healthcare system, infant mortality rates are up because of a lack of prenatal care. The life expectancy was 79 years prior to the dissolution of the U.S., now the life expectancy rate for the former U.S. dropped to 76 within two years! That is a dramatic drop. That usually only happens in countries experiencing famines, plagues, or wars. In every category of treatable diseases, the survival rates have decreased. The dissolution of the U.S. has been horrible for our health.

The poverty rate has increased as well, and that has a direct correlation to the drop in life expectancy.

What about the psychological toll?

Unfortunately, the national suicide rate has increased dramatically, as well as substance abuse. Again, it especially affected the poor, but in every demographic, the rates have increased.

What do you attribute to those increases in suicide and substance abuse?

Despair, hopelessness, severe depression. Look, humans crave stability, and the U.S. was one of the most stable nations in the world despite all of our problems with mass shootings and the fentanyl crisis. Now it's gone. People took it for granted that it would always be there and then it wasn't. That takes a huge toll on your psyche. For everyone over two years old, for most Americans (former), the U.S. was their home and part of their identity. Think about losing part of your identity. Couple that with the huge economic downturn. Folks losing their jobs and healthcare. Americans' healthcare was tied to their jobs. The collapse of the U.S. has had this cascading negative effect on our health.

Do you see it getting better?

Like I said, there are rays of hope with Native American tribes working together to provide healthcare to their people. It is a formula that can be emulated. But I do not expect things to get better for many, many years. Unless you can afford it, you can no longer take for granted access to 21st-century healthcare.

(LOS GATOS, CA, OUTSIDE OF SAN JOSE, CA) FRAN GIBBONS, NETCINEMA DIRECTOR OF PROGRAMMING

Mr. Gibbons, you have been in the entertainment industry for over 30 years. You have worked for a traditional network and a movie studio as well as multiple online platforms. How has the entertainment industry been affected by the collapse of the U.S.?

It really depends upon which sector you are talking about. With the huge economic downturn when the U.S. dissolved, the platforms and networks that rely on advertising tanked. Many of them went out of business. Shoot, two out of three major networks filed for bankruptcy. That is unprecedented. Companies could no longer afford to advertise. Every sector of the economy was negatively affected except for gun and ammo sales. Go figure. So, it naturally affected the entertainment industry. Also, our customers had less discretionary income, so the movie theater industry never fully recovered from the COVID pandemic. Besides some independent movie theaters, most others closed down. Try to find a movie theater in San Jose right now. Good luck!

What about the streaming services like yours?

We started showing ads in 2022, but we also offered a no-ad service that you had to pay for. Ads right now represent about 10% of our revenue so we did take a big hit when we had a huge drop in ad sales, but fortunately, Netcinema started without ads, so we were okay. A lot of other streaming services were not okay, and many went under. Streaming services are now the domain of only a few big names. It is almost like the big three networks back in the day.

There have been accusations that the remaining streaming services have banded together to agree on pricing and that, overall, the quantity and quality of content has gone down. How do you answer those allegations?

There is absolutely no truth to the "price fixing." The market dictates the pricing for our services, and all the major streaming service levels have to follow the same market. Of course, our prices would be similar.

But how can you explain the almost doubling of a monthly subscription in the past two years?

Since the U.S. dissolved, prices for everything went up dramatically. Making high-quality content is not cheap. Labor costs, especially with big-name actors, have skyrocketed along with everything associated with making movies. Those juicy tax breaks we used to get from certain states to lure us into filming there are gone. The former states are now scrambling to raise revenue any way they can, and so taxes in the #1 way.

As far as the quality and quantity of content going down, I will agree that the sheer quantity of original material has gone down drastically. We just cannot afford it anymore, and as far as the quality, that is in the eye of the beholder! You still have your membership, right?

(WASHINGTON, DC CITY HALL) MAYOR KENYA BALLY

Mayor Bally, what has it been like as the leader of a city that is the seat of power for the most powerful nation in human history that is coming apart and now no longer exists?

Wow, that is a loaded question, and the answer is very emotional and complicated. First, Washington, DC, is still the capital of the U.S., or what is left of it. We still have most of the institutions, but in many cases, it is like they are ghosts or a shadow of what they once were. Just think about the tax base that powered the U.S. government. In 2023, the federal government collected $4.44 trillion.[14] That number has been cut by over 80%. Prior to the collapse of the U.S., Washington, DC, was funded by Congress and the federal government. One we had 37 states break away, Washington, DC, gained statehood. It is a mixed blessing. On the one hand, we now have voting members of both houses of Congress. On the other hand, we now must fend for ourselves financially.

The trappings of the U.S. are still present throughout DC, but there have been significant cuts. Take, for example, the Smithsonian museums. Prior to the dissolution of the U.S., there were 17 museums, galleries, and a zoo that comprised the Smithsonian Institution that were all free to the public and open every day of the year except for Christmas Day.[15]

We are now down to six, and all of them charge for entrance and have limited hours. And the most popular Smithsonian facility, the zoo, is on life support. I could give several other examples, such as some parks that the federal government oversaw, but the list is extensive.

Also, our population has dropped by 15% since the collapse. Since Washington, DC, is no longer the capital of the most powerful country in the world, foreign embassies have cut their staff significantly, and also every four years migration of people in and out has dropped drastically.

Furthermore, the crime rate has continued to rise. Our murder rate was already problematic before the U.S. ceased to exist. The drop in jobs, as well as the budget cutbacks for violence mitigation

---

[14]"How much revenue has the U.S. government collected this year?" Fiscal Date.Treasury.gov, accessed on May 24, 2024, https://fiscaldata.treasury.gov/americas-finance-guide/government-revenue/.
[15]"Smithsonian Museums in Washington DC," Washington, DC.org, accessed on May 24, 2024, https://washington.org/smithsonian-institution-museums.

programs, has created the perfect storm. Back in the eighties and nineties, DC was dubbed the "murder capital" of the world. I hope we do not go back to that moniker.

The vignettes above were intended to show the breadth and width of the consequences of a collapse of the U.S. Again, it is not intended to be a prediction but a starting point for understanding what we have to lose.

Germany, a Cautionary Tale

Writers must be very careful and sensitive when comparing and contrasting the events in Germany during the middle of the 20th century to current events, but it is worth revisiting. I heard it said that history does not repeat itself, but it does often rhyme (the author of this statement is in dispute).[16] Germany during World War II is at least worth showing as an example of what can happen when extreme views and rhetoric morph into actions, embracing outlandish, dangerous conspiracy theories such as Jews are the root of all evil and there is a worldwide Jewish conspiracy to subjugate the German people; Germany didn't lose World War I, it was the Kaiser and the Jews, and Hitler is some kind of messiah.

I have had significant experience in Germany. My father was born in Germany on January 31, 1929, and was raised under National Socialism. He was in the Hitler Youth and attended an Adolf Hitler Schule (12 total throughout Germany). Students were specially selected for their intelligence, athleticism, and adherence to the values of National Socialism.[17] He was groomed to be part of the future Nazi elite and bureaucracy. Fortunately, the war ended when he was 18 and preparing to enter that world (the irony is that my biological mother is Jewish). I have spent my adult life trying to understand how a country with such a rich culture of the arts, science, and medicine could condone and embrace those Nazi ideals. Growing up in the South and attending The Citadel, the Military College of South Carolina, I have done the same mental gymnastics over how Confederate Army officers who had taken an oath to support and defend the U.S. Constitution could violate it and fight their brothers. My father refused to ever talk about growing up under

---

[16]"History Does Repeat Itself, But It Does Rhyme," Quote Investigator, January 12, 2014, https://quoteinvestigator.com/2014/01/12/history-rhymes/.
[17]"National Socialist Training School for the Party Elite [Ordensburg] in Sonthofen, Allgäu (1939)," German History in Documents and Images (GHDI), accessed on May 24, 2024, https://ghdi.ghi-dc.org/sub_image.cfm?image_id=1903&language=english.

National Socialism, so I researched it on my own. I lived in Germany off and on for ten years, learned the language, and made it a point to visit most concentration camps, World War I and World War II battlefields, Allied and German cemeteries, sites of mass extermination (outside Vilnius, Lithuania and Babar Yar in Kiev), and history museums across all of Europe from France to Ukraine, the Balkans, and the Baltics. My conclusions are:

-Conclusion #1: The German population all knew about the atrocities a few years after Hitler came to power. National events like Kristallnacht could not be ignored. German mass-produced radios and even sent mobile theaters to remote German villages without electricity. If you think the German population was not complicit, visit the Flosssenberg concentration camp near the Czech border. The camp sits in the middle of the town at the very bottom of a valley surrounded by the town.[18] Almost every home had a clear view of the barracks and the open areas. Not knowing was unavoidable. Finally, think of it this way, if your neighbor and his entire family two doors down disappeared in the middle of the night, never to be heard from again, and a new family moved in, would you not have heard about it? Or if your favorite independent bookstore was burned to the ground while firemen watched. People talk. There was no way for the German population, even in remote areas, not to know what was going on.

Conclusion #2: the vast majority of humans are capable of committing or turning a blind eye to unspeakable acts against their fellow humans. That is the cautionary tale for current events. The resurgence of the far right, Holocaust deniers, etc. Even just ignoring what they are saying because you share similar beliefs in other areas is a slippery slope and legitimizes and desensitizes their dangerous behavior and ideals. I saw the results of this first-hand in the immediate aftermath of the war in Bosnia from 1996-1999 while deployed there as part of the NATO peacekeeping mission.

What does this have to do with current events in the U.S.? It shows that democracies are both resilient and fragile, and when one loses faith and trust in institutions and demonizes your fellow citizens, it can easily fall. And by the time the citizenry takes the threat seriously, it is too late.

---

[18]"Flossenberg Concentration Camp website, accessed May 24, 2024, https://www.gedenkstaette-flossenbuerg.de/en/.

Part of the U.S.'s divisions are a result of both sides not listening to the other. It can be hard to really identify core issues, valid concerns, and genuine solutions amidst all the venomous rancor. At its core, all sides want the U.S. to succeed and want what they think is best for our country. You really have to pay attention to what others are saying and try and set aside (or tamp down) the raw emotions to understand.

I have grown to respect and understand some of the valid concerns of those in the Trump movement, even though I do not like the way it is packaged or described in absolute terms. After almost 80 years of the U.S. being the world's policeman, our people are tired of it. We are tired and frustrated with bailing out other countries with very little appreciation. I was applying for a UN job many years ago. The position was custom-built for me and read like my resume. While I was going through the process, the U.S. State Department contacted me through a little-known office, The UN Employment Information and Assistance Unit, which assists Americans who are applying for jobs in international organizations.[19] I asked them why the U.S. needs an office dedicated to helping Americans get UN jobs. They told me that even though the U.S. provides 22% of the UN budget, we are severely underrepresented at the UN. Asia and Africa have a stranglehold on UN jobs and the hiring process.[20] I was surprised but not surprised. My point is that my situation is just a small example of how the U.S. gives much to the world and sometimes does not get much back. By the way, I did not get the job.

I am concerned about a completely isolationist approach, though. The U.S. was called to the continent of Europe twice in the 20th century. We stayed there afterward as a bulwark against the Soviet Union. Worldwide, we were also policing the web of international agreements and organizations that we helped establish after World War II. That interlocking network kept the peace and prevented World War III. Is it time for the U.S. to reevaluate our position and commitments in the world? Probably, but withdrawal from European affairs is not the way to go, especially with a revanchist Russia. Plus, if your neighbor's house is on fire, do you ignore it? Eventually that fire will spread.

---

[19]"Employment Opportunities with the United Nations and Other International Organizations," U.S. State Department Archive, accessed on May 24, 2024, Employment Opportunities with the United Nations and Other International Organizations (state.gov).

[20]"Personnel by Nationality," UN Chief Executives Board for Coordination (CEB), accessed on May 24, 2024, https://unsceb.org/hr-nationality.

Some of the social justice turmoil on both sides is concerning. Banning books is an anathema to our American identity. Free speech is enshrined in our Constitution. Also, concerns are not just valid as long as its subjects or opinions that do not make you comfortable. The "shouting down" or canceling of conservative lecturers and visitors on left-leaning campuses is just as repugnant to the right as book banning is to the left.

Some of the culture wars are also concerning, such as the striking down of Roe vs. Wade by the U.S. Supreme Court. Many women see it as a woman's health care issue and a very personal decision. According to the CDC, in 2020, there were 11.2 abortions per 1000 women ages 15 to 44, and 25% of all U.S. women will have an abortion by the end of their childbearing years.[21] It touches every segment of society, every race, and both conservatives and liberals alike. Does it really need to be a political issue or more a personal decision like the deeply personal choice of religious worship?

Ridiculing someone else's culture, beliefs, or background and using it as a punchline is not a way to engender understanding either. All it does is build resentment. The left's ridicule of gun culture or rural, white males is just as toxic as the right's ridicule of the concerns of those in the Black Lives Matter movement or sensitivities over someone's choice in how they gender identify. You do not have to accept someone else's views that you think ludicrous, but you should at least show basic respect towards them.

It is this lack of friendship that can erode a society. When basic common courtesies such as respectfully listening to those whose opinions differ from yours become rare and seen as a sign of weakness, then we need to take a hard look at ourselves in the mirror.

Extremism of either side, left or right, is not good and goes counter to the American way of governance, which requires compromise to function, and that compromise often (in the past at least) leads to centrist decisions, legislation, etc. The right's fetishization of strongmen throughout the world is concerning. I know from personal experience that the only thing that bullies and autocrats fear and respect is power and those who stand up against them. Just look at the hoops Russian President Putin went through to silence the deceased dissident, Alexei Navalny.

***

[21]Margot Sanger-Katz, Claire Cain Miller and Quoctrung Bui, "Who Gets Abortions in America?" *New York Times*, December 14, 2021, https://www.nytimes.com/interactive/2021/12/14/upshot/who-gets-abortions-in-america.html?smid=nytcore-android-share.

Ben Franklin (a case for a time traveler if there ever was one) was asked by a lady at the end of the Constitutional Convention in 1787, "Doctor, what have we got a republic or a monarchy?" Dr. Franklin replied, "A republic if we can keep it."[22]

This story is just a work of fiction, but the chances of it happening are more than 0%. I have watched democracies fail throughout the world and have watched them recover. What is happening now in the U.S. is very alarming and concerning. Instead of just disagreeing with our fellow Americans over key issues of the day and arguing over points of culture that every generation fights over, we have demonized those we do not agree with. The current fights are a zero-sum game where if your side loses an issue, it is a catastrophe or an existential crisis. Instead of developing a better argument, modifying a stance, or compromising, we instead make it out to be a loss on the scale of losing a war. Our responses are disproportionate to the silliness of the issues in many cases.

There are rays of hope, though. When the U.S. catches a cold, the world sneezes. I think it can also be the other way around. Many countries around the world are rejecting hard left and right views. Poland, which was ruled by a hard-right government that banned abortion and sought to neuter the independence of the judiciary, elected a central government. In Brazil, their equivalent of January 6th was soundly rejected and repudiated throughout society. Germany is rejecting the resurgence of a far-right, anti-immigration movement. Japan has managed to maintain a relatively conservative culture without the cultural war divisions that other countries have faced.

The U.S. has faced seemingly unfixable divisions in the past, prior to the Civil War, during the Depression and the isolationist movement, and the divisive sixties. What has been the solution? That answer is complicated. It is usually a unifying event like the Civil War, World War II, or the Iran hostage situation. It is when we Americans reach the brink and a point of exhaustion. But it usually involves an informed and engaged citizenry who understands the need to compromise for our country to function.

---

[22]Julie Miller, "A republic if you can keep it: Elizabeth Willing Powel, Benjamin Franklin, and the James McHenry Journal," Library of Congress Blogs, January 6, 2022,
Posted by: Julie Miller https://blogs.loc.gov/manuscripts/2022/01/a-republic-if-you-can-keep-it-elizabeth-willing-powel-benjamin-franklin-and-the-james-mchenry-journal/.

Americans need to keep in mind that Amazon is still delivering, the International Space Station is still orbiting with an international crew to includes Russians, disputes in NFL games are still parsed with a level of detail normally reserved for a commercial plane crash, and you do not have to worry about government officials breaking into your house in the middle of the night and taking away a family member.

Our government is going through a stress test and divisions that we have never experienced. It is unchartered territory. Our Founding Fathers knew they could not anticipate every major problem our country would face, but they did develop a constitution adaptable enough and with the right "checks and balances" for unforeseeable challenges; as long as all participants played by the rules written and unwritten. It starts with treating our fellow countrymen as humans with the same desire to have a country that is safe and open and gives everyone the same chances to have a fruitful life.

David Brooks wrote a series of columns about how we have lost a layer of society and interaction that forced us to have regular, normal interactions with people outside of our tribe.[23] The Republican is interacting with the Democrats both participating in their child's PTA. Or the neighborhood get-togethers in Charleston, South Carolina, where you interact with the immigrant family from Pakistan as well as the couple who just moved from New York City. Those innocent interactions humanize our fellow countrymen. Civic and fraternal organizations have seen a drastic drop in membership. I am a veteran and in previous wars, it was typical for returning veterans to join their local chapter of the Veterans of Foreign Wars (VFW). I have not joined any fraternal organization. You can blame it on social media and cell phones, but it does not replace face-to-face interaction with people outside of our tribe.

I straddle both worlds. I am from South Carolina, a military veteran, and a white middle-aged man. But I am also the son of a first-generation immigrant and have a Jewish biological mother. Like most American families, mine is a mix of contradictions. I work in government/military circles where conservatism is prevalent. I also have children who go to arguably the two most liberal universities in the U.S. My mother cried when Bush, Jr. was reelected. My father, who was raised in Germany during the 1930s, admired the earlier version of Vladimir Putin. I see the hardline

[23]David Brooks, "Building a community is hard but more crucial than ever," *The New York Times*, May 17, 2016, https://www.sandiegouniontribune.com/opinion/commentary/sdut-david-brooks-community-column-2016may17-story.html.

stance on both sides. I could argue for the development of a third party, but our two-party system is so entrenched that unless there is a once-in-a-generation charismatic leader who coalesces around a single issue, I do not see it happening. As previously stated, what has worked in the past to bring us together is an existential crisis or institutions and organizations that put people together who normally would not associate with each other working towards a common goal. Sports, the military, and academics are the best examples. I recommend expanding, requiring, or incentivizing those organizations and causes that require us to work together at the local and national levels. Organizations like:

- Teach for America
- PTAs
- The military
- AmeriCorps
- Church mission trips within the borders of the U.S.

These programs already exist, but there needs to be an expansion and more incentives, such as exemption from taxes while participating or a guarantee of a college degree or a technical certification. The bar to enter must be easier, and incentives need to be more compelling and simpler to understand. Many people get turned off by the bureaucracy it takes to enter a program. Let's say you can enter an AmeriCorps program for 18 months, go to a location in need that is based on your top five choices, teaches you're a tangible skill like electrician, coder, or EMT while you work, pays you a salary, provides for living expenses, and is tax free. Or, as an adult already established in your career, it provides an incentive to get involved in local government or an organization like the PTA.

Whatever we do, it will have to be a conscious decision and require action. Democracy requires citizens to act, autocracies do not. America seems to be at its best when we combine grassroots activism with big government muscle. It is not naïve to suggest this. Just look at the U.S. during the 1930s. Organizations like the Civilian Conservation Corps helped bring people together from across the country and create parks, etc. that are still present today. America is good at big ideas.

Unfortunately, any American over 30 years old will rarely change their views. Remember the old saying from the sixties: never trust anyone over 30? We must focus on generational change and the youth today. In schools, we should require civics lessons that teach our youth to be discerning consumers of information as well as grasp the basic concepts of how our government works. I am constantly amazed at the members of the U.S. Congress who do not comprehend that the Founding Fathers intentionally established three branches of government with checks and balances where each branch had the power to check the other branches. No branch holds more power than others. This system forces compromise and as stated before, naturally lends itself to governance from the center and not the extremes. These civics courses should also teach students to question everything they hear and develop their own informed opinions from multiple sources with different views.

Furthermore, they should understand that democracy requires active participation from an informed citizenry based on stated and implied customs and norms of civility. Many high schools today require volunteer work to graduate. I think volunteerism is a great idea, and the students should be required to work in areas that are out of their comfort zone. Familiarity breeds compassion. That means new experiences coupled with a balanced approach to education.

America has not failed or collapsed yet. I have repeated this mantra often in a wager involving the U.S.; betting for the U.S. is always a safe bet. But maintaining democracies requires active participation and care. Indifference can lead to its demise. The U.S. is still the destination for those lacking hope throughout the world. Just look at our southern border. There are a lot of mothers and fathers who have risked it all for the promise of a better life in the U.S. I have spent the past 18 months in Ukraine helping train their military in their existential fight against the Russians. A Ukrainian friend, fixer, lawyer, etc., spent two years in the U.S. as a young man working at an amusement park. It was miserable work. The hours were horrible, the pay crap, and the living conditions cramped. He had to sit in a hot box making popcorn for snooty tourists. He bought a used car with his cousin, and at night, they would drive for a ride-hailing service. He was in the U.S. during the 2016 election, so he got a front row seat to our dysfunction. When I asked him what he thought of the U.S. after that experience, he told me that the U.S. is still the greatest country in the world because you can make something of yourself from nothing. The problem is that Americans take it for granted and do not know what they could be missing.

The key takeaways from my journey of discovery are the following:

- Extremes and binary choices are like ultimatums; they rarely work, and there are ALWAYS unintended negative consequences
- Positive change will have to be generational, and anyone over 30 is a lost cause
- Education and new experiences will be the difference
- Hope is not a course of action (this phrase is constantly said in military circles)
- Almost anyone is capable of doing horrendous things to other humans, given the right set of circumstances.
- It has always been a safe wager betting on the U.S. and Americans
- Led Zeppelin is the world's greatest rock & roll band
- Van Halen sucked without David Lee Roth

Strong democracies are remarkably resilient, but weak democracies are fragile. The U.S. democracy has strengthened since its infancy and weathered several crises which could have easily caused its demise. The tipping point for the collapse of the U.S. and the possible scenarios are impossible to predict. I have strived to keep the scenarios as grounded in reality as much as possible. One plausible scenario is what happens if Trump wins the presidency, is sworn in as president, and then is found guilty of criminal charges in Georgia and sentenced to prison. What happens next?

The Ukrainians have a patriotic saying, *"Glory to Ukraine (Slava Ukraini),"* and the response is *"Glory to the Heroes (Heroiam slava)."* The U.S. should be, *"Glory to the American Republic"; "If we can keep it together."*

Made in the USA
Monee, IL
20 December 2024

32d83d49-eb35-44dd-8303-2fe0df053fb4R01